DEAD
GET ~~WELL~~ SOON.

Most novelists take a vacation when they finish a book. Writer Lyon Wentworth preferred to solve mysteries instead. This time it was the suspicious scalding death of his wife Bea's favorite teacher, Fabian Bunting. But old Faby was only the first victim to find herself in hot water. A labor dispute at the Murphysville Convalescent Home had heated up into violence, and one bizarre murder after another was leading right to Yew Corner, the mansion of the Home's beautiful owner, Serena Truman.

So that's where Bea and Lyon were going to dinner—a special dinner arranged by Serena, where every guest had a perfect motive to kill. Now it was Lyon's job to spot the culprit, preferably over cocktails...before death could serve up another unexpected corpse.

The Death at Yew Corner

Richard Forrest

A DELL BOOK

For Senator Mary Faye Brumby

Published by
Dell Publishing Co., Inc.
1 Dag Hammarskjold Plaza
New York, New York 10017

Dell® TM 681510, Dell Publishing Co., Inc.

ISBN: 0-440-11782-8

Reprinted by arrangement with Holt, Rinehart and Winston, CBS
Educational and Professional Publishing

Printed in the United States of America

First Dell printing—September 1984

DD

1

"DON'T LET the goddamn scabs in here. Hit him with a two-by-four!"

"Faby, please! Dottie is trying to rest and you're upsetting her."

Fabian Bunting ignored the comment, gripped the window frame tightly, and continued looking down out the window of the Murphysville Convalescent Home at the picket line of strikers one floor below. "There's a fink trying the side door. Get him!"

"Faby, if you don't stop I'll have to sedate you. We can't have you throwing the pin out of your hip."

"You just try that, hon. I'll jam the hypodermic in your fanny." The old woman shrugged the nurse's restraining hand from her shoulder. "And in the future, young woman, you may call me Bunting. Dr. Bunting. And for your information, the individual in the other bed is Mrs. Rathbone."

"We can't have this! Really!" The nurse wheeled the casement window shut, latched it, and firmly pushed Fabian Bunting back in her wheelchair. "I'm sorry there isn't any OT today, but with most of the staff out it can't be helped."

"Why aren't you on the picket line, sweets?"

"I'm a professional." The nurse straightened her carriage and aligned the fall of her skirt. "Now, please be good. We're terribly shorthanded and . . ."

"What do I get if I'm good?"

"Well, I'll find you something nice. Perhaps a special dessert treat with lunch."

"A treat? Jesus! Do you think I'm suffering from anility, Miss Whatever-your-name-is?"

"Miss Williams."

"Do you know what the word means?" The old woman peered closely at the name tag on the nurse's blouse. "Bambi. God, a grown woman named Bambi."

Miss Williams turned on her heels and flounced from the small room. Fabian Bunting spun her wheelchair in a semicircle. "It's the feminine form of senility, Bambi," she called. "The word has an interesting derivation. It's from the Latin *anilis*, meaning old woman. Old woman," she repeated again under her breath. She wanted to throw things, to throw something against the wall. She wanted to hear the breaking of glass to assuage the hurt that filled her. But most of all, she wanted to break the binds of her physical self that had brought her here after eighty-four years of thriving independence. Her hand brushed vehemently along the bureau, knocking cosmetics and assorted bottles to the tile floor where they shattered into dozens of shards. It made her feel a little better.

"Miz Bunting, please don't make so much noise."

Faby Bunting whirled her wheelchair to face the other bed, which was occupied by a frail woman younger than herself. There was a poignant quality to the plea. It was a note of desperation from someone who could voice no other. "I'm sorry, Mrs. Rathbone."

"I never did like loud noises," the wavering voice said in a plea of a different sort.

"I guess you didn't, dear," Fabian said in a compassionate tone. "I seem to get very angry recently. I get mad at all sorts of things, worthy or not. Do you know what I mean? I've got to feel, and God only knows there isn't much in here to laugh about."

"I only want to be quiet and sleep."

I know you do, Faby thought. You've already stopped eating and you hardly speak. I think you've chosen your time. She turned back to the dresser and bent forward to open the middle drawer. What she was looking for was at the back, and she rummaged until she found the small case. The leather was old and cracked, but the opera glasses were still serviceable. She wheeled out the door and down the hall.

She looked down at the opera glasses in her lap and she remembered that she'd bought them in Paris. The year? Oh, God, let her remember the year. 1930. Yes, 1930, the year she'd gone to the Sorbonne for postdoctoral work. It had been a fabulous year of talk in the cafés, love, and passion. What had become of Max? Dead. Like all the others now gone. Pity.

The long hall that bisected the length of the second floor of the convalescent home was empty. As she wheeled past the nurses' station at the hallway's midpoint, she noticed that it was vacant. The strike hurt. They were running their asses off. Good!

No one was in the sun-room at the far end of the building. She wheeled across the tiles toward the bank of windows overlooking the parking lot and right flank of the picket line. She raised the opera glasses and swept them across her field of vision. A covey of strikers surrounded a tall, black woman who seemed to be giving directions. Fabian remembered her. On her last visit, Bea Wentworth had introduced her to the union organizer. The name? She must always struggle to remember. Ward. Yes, Kimberly Ward.

A four-door sedan filled with six or seven men and women moved slowly down the road and turned toward the parking lot. More scabs. Newly hired workers brought to replace the strikers. Kim wouldn't let them get through. She saw the black woman shouting, pointing, and now taking a position in front of the slowly moving car as other strikers surrounded the vehicle and rocked it from side to side. A striker was pounding on the windshield with his sign. They wouldn't get by. Good!

Something was going on immediately below the sun-room windows. Along the side wall of the building was a small courtyard enclosed on three sides by a high brick wall that usually contained the home's station wagon and dumpster. The van parked there this morning was unfamiliar. Its rear door was open and three men stood nearby arguing.

She watched them with the opera glasses. It was impossible to tell what they were saying, but it was obvious that two of the men were in a violent fight with a third. Her knuckles turned white as her grip on the glasses tightened. One of the men pinned the arms of the second while the third hit him. The victim doubled forward and fell to the pavement where he lay on his side. She could see a small trickle of blood ooze from his right ear. The unconscious man was lifted and thrown into the rear of the van.

The van backed out of the courtyard and turned into the parking lot. The vehicle accelerated as it approached the picket line. The strikers parted before the rushing vehicle as it left the convalescent home property and turned up the street.

One man remained in the courtyard. He waited until the van cleared the line of strikers before he turned toward the building. She noticed that he wore hospital whites.

As the hunted will be furtive, the man in the courtyard glanced in either direction and then up. Their eyes made contact. Fabian Bunting lowered her glasses and placed them on the windowsill. She swiveled her chair and began to propel herself down the long, vacant hall.

There was a phone at the nurses' station. She would dial 911. Surely someone would be interested in what she had just seen.

She pushed the wheels as fast as she could but felt them spin from her hands. She turned to see a man behind her firmly gripping the handles of her chair.

"Let me go!"

He didn't answer. She lurched forward when the chair made a sharp right-angle turn. He had swiveled the chair directly toward the double swinging doors of the physical therapy room. The doors swung shut behind them, and she felt a strong hand clamp over her mouth. The fingers smelled of tobacco.

He pushed her across the room until the front of the chair

bumped against the galvanized surface of a raised whirlpool tub. The hand that pressed against her mouth increased its pressure until her head slammed back against the headrest. The man bent forward and used his free hand to twirl a faucet valve.

Steam rose as scalding water rushed into the tub.

She looked up into the face of the man holding her not in fright so much as wonderment. She didn't expect her system could tolerate much, but she wondered why. Yes, why?

It would have been interesting to know.

BEA WENTWORTH AWOKE in a funk.

She opened one eye to peer up at her husband who was standing over her with a cup and saucer. It was unusual for him to bring her coffee in bed. He must have sensed her mood. She turned and opened the other eye to watch as he set the coffee gently on the night table.

She could have predicted his dress before she saw him: a loose-fitting sport shirt that was color-uncoordinated with rumpled khaki pants, canvas boat shoes, and no socks. For the first time, his lack of appropriate footwear annoyed her.

"There're clean socks in your drawer."

"Uh huh. Coffee?"

She sat up and held the cup in both hands. "You're the only person in the world who can wrinkle fresh wash and wear."

"You've forgotten our rule. You are never to speak until you've had your first morning coffee."

"Good rule." She drank and felt a warmth spread through her, causing a mild uplifting of her spirits. She drank again and watched Lyon lean against the wall with a bemused expression on his face. No socks and all, she liked the way he looked. He was a tall, angular, fortyish man. His blond-browning hair fell over his forehead, and he often pushed it back with a nonchalant palm. His smile had faded into a slightly troubled look, but she knew that his features could shift instantaneously to a wide, warm smile.

"You going to work in the garden today?" he asked.

5

"It's going to rain."

"You could return the governor's call."

"Have."

He took the cup from her hand and sipped coffee. "And?"

"She offered me a job."

A smile broke across his face. If she hadn't been so irritable, she would have kissed him.

"That's great! Why don't you take it until you start your next campaign?"

"I may never run for office again."

"Sorry for ourselves this morning, aren't we?"

"The governor wants me to serve on a committee that's investigating legalized gambling."

He looked a little dubious. "Well, that could be interesting."

"I may be against legalized gambling entirely."

"Investigating it is one way to find out. Or you could take that Washington offer."

"No thanks. An under-under secretary on the civil service commission is burial."

Lyon looked at his wife with concern. The bulky quilt mostly hid her tallish, well-proportioned figure, but he knew well the trim curves of her body. He wanted to run his hands through her close-cropped hair, but this didn't seem to be a terribly auspicious time. Her dark eyes were usually darting and energetic, filled with bright perception and humor. This morning they seemed listless. His wife's vitality had temporarily vanished, but he knew it would return. She would eventually recover from her recent election defeat. In the meantime, he wished there was something he could do to lighten her depression.

"Suppose we take a trip to New York. We could stay a few days and take in a couple of shows."

She smiled for the first time that morning. "You're nearly finished with the book. Maybe when it's done we can go to the city and celebrate." She pushed up from the bed. "I'm alive now. Thanks for the coffee."

She rinsed breakfast dishes, placed them on the rack in the dishwasher, and then looked out the window into a misty morning. The day wouldn't entice her into the garden. She could faintly hear the steady *pickity pock* of Lyon's typewriter in the study. The steady rhythm of the typing told her that the book was going well. In a few days her husband's benign children's monsters, the Wobblies, would again sally forth to deal in more adventure and good deeds.

God, that's what she needed. Her own personal Wobbly to ward off the demons of depression. Bea slammed the dishwasher shut and turned the operating dial. She must keep busy. She must fill her days until the personal demons disappeared and life's color returned.

Bea drove the pickup truck toward the town of Murphysville. She had decided to visit Fabian Bunting. She laughed aloud. Fabian's iconoclastic outlook on life, and the vibrancy of the old woman, would put her depression in its proper perspective. She could almost predict what her old teacher would say: "For God's sake, Beatrice, cut the self-pity. You've taught, served in the state house of representatives, state senate, and a term as secretary of the state. So, you lost a congressional election to a man far to the right of Joe McCarthy . . . go sulk, honey." Yes, Faby would make her laugh again, and Bea knew that her duty visit to the Murphysville Convalescent Home would do more for her than for the patient.

She'd go as soon as she did some shopping at the supermarket. The visit would be a needed remedy for a bleak day overshadowed with dark uncertainties that occasionally haunted midlife.

Murphysville, Connecticut, was located near the geographical center of the state, thirty miles southeast of Hartford. It was a town that in many ways appeared to be untouched by the past hundred years. The village green still faced a circle of homes, churches, and stores whose façades, by edict of the historical commission, had remained the same since the turn of the century. A mile down Main Street, away from the green, Bea pulled into a small shopping center. She purchased groceries and then continued on for another mile toward the outskirts of town and the convalescent home.

Activity on the picket line stretched across the front of the home was now desultory. The strikers seemed to be conserving energy as they waited for the next shift change when they would again attempt to intimidate those still working in the home. Two men walked slowly abreast with militant placards, while most of the others had spread out across the grass and held Styrofoam cups of coffee.

Kim Ward was talking animatedly to several workers as Bea parked her car up the street and walked toward her. The black woman had been Bea's assistant for the past several years, first in the legislature, then during Bea's term as secretary of the state. She had been Bea's campaign manager for her last disastrous campaign for Congress. Now, her former aide and friend was an organizer for the newly formed service workers union.

Kim smiled and waved as Bea crossed the grass and walked toward her. "Hey, Bea! You here to give moral support or join the line?"

"None of the above. I'm stopping in to see Dr. Bunting for a few minutes."

"We've heard that one before," a heavyset woman stretched out on the grass with obviously painful feet said belligerently. "They give us that jazz and then sneak in and empty bedpans."

"Senator Wentworth's all right," another striker said.

Bea held up both hands. "Honest, no work, no bedpans, no mopping. One short visit to an old lady friend and teacher."

"That's the one who hung out the window this morning and yelled, 'Right on.' "

"Bunting's a tiger," someone added.

Bea waved, promised to return later to hear their grievances, and walked briskly down the short walk to the main entrance of the home. There was no one at the reception desk near the door. A glance down the corridors revealed them to be empty also.

She decided to take the stairs for one flight rather than wait for the slow self-service elevator. She hurried up the stairwell as if hoping to avoid the all-pervasive smell of the place. She detested this building and well understood why Fabian Bunting fought it with every fiber of her being. It was a mirror of the future—a future filled with Bea's own limitations and the inexorable march of old age. Her present depression told her that youth was past, which meant that age hovered around a nearby corner. Infirmity crept so stealthily that you were not aware of it until it was too late for conscious choice or action.

The stairway's exit on the second floor was directly in front of the nurses' station. A harried R.N. glanced up myopically at Bea and then back down to her medicine tray. Another nurse rushed from one side of the hall to a room across the way in answer to some plea. Bea turned to the left toward Dr. Bunting's room, which was the fifth door down from the nurses' station.

She knocked softly on the open door and stepped inside. Dr. Bunting's bed by the window was empty. The bedding was still rumpled from the night before.

A frail old woman curled up in a fetal position in the near bed blinked her eyes open and stared at Bea.

"Is Dr. Bunting around?"

"She makes so much noise" was the whining response.

Bea laughed. "I imagine she does. I'm Bea Wentworth, Mrs. Rathbone. We met last week. You told me about your children."

"I have four you know."

"Yes, and I know you're very proud of them."

"I'm going to die."

Bea did not know how to respond to that statement. She had no way of knowing the actual physical condition of the old woman, her mental stability, or the power of her will—which she suspected had ebbed away. "I thought you were looking better today" was her reply.

"No, I'm not. The loud one went down the hall in her chair. She probably went to the sun-room."

"Yes, thank you. Perhaps we can talk later."

"That would be nice." The reply was nearly lost as the old woman closed her eyes and clutched a blanket to her neck.

Bea hurried from the room with a twinge of shame, not really knowing how to cope with the situation. How should she react to a woman willing herself to die? She realized that Dr. Bunting's verbose battle against infirmity and incompetence indicated a fierce will to live.

The R.N. at the nurses' station looked up as Bea passed. "Can I help you?"

"I'm looking for Fabian Bunting."

"I think she went to the sun-room." The nurse looked back at her charts.

Bea stood in the doorway of the empty sun-room. A midmorning sun had forced its way through protesting clouds and fell in irregular columns across the floor tiles. The imitation leather-covered chairs with chrome fittings shone dully in the dusty light. She walked to the far windowsill and picked up the opera glasses resting there. She held them in the palm of her hand for a moment, and then slowly put them back and walked to the nurses' station.

"Dr. Bunting is not in the sun-room."

The R.N. glanced up and scowled. "I can't keep track of every patient by myself. We are shorthanded, you know?"

"I know you are, and it must be difficult. Perhaps she is somewhere else in the building?"

"Well, how would I . . . ?" The nurse gave a shrug of resignation and grabbed a chart. "She's not charted for anything. She could have gone to the OT room, the TV room, or she might be visiting another patient. I just don't have the time."

"Thank you." Bea turned away. She had been in the convalescent home a dozen times since it opened three years ago. She had known other patients here, and since Dr. Bunting's admission, had visited at least once a week. The layout of the home was simple: a two-story brick building with the main wing parallel to the street and two side wings running toward the rear of the property from each end of the main building. There was a construction site at the rear of the property that would eventually be an annex containing additional beds. The wings contained kitchens, offices, service areas, and a laundry. The game room was downstairs alongside the occupational therapy room. She would try there first.

In twenty minutes she had established that Fabian was not in any of the common rooms, nor was she visiting another patient. A vague sense of alarm quickened her pace as she went back to the nurses' station on the second floor.

The R.N. she had spoken to earlier was pushing a medicine cart at the far end of the corridor. Bea slouched against the counter of the station to wait. Of course, it was silly to worry. Bunting was the kind of person who might have gone anywhere . . . wheelchair or not. She could possibly be back in the kitchens complaining about the food, or in the laundry room.

Across the hall were double swinging doors. A small black-and-white plaque announced the entrance to the physical therapy room. The nurse was not yet halfway down the hall. Bea walked impatiently toward the double doors and pushed them open.

Curls of steam rose from a galvanized tub in the far corner of the PT room. A hand with talonlike fingers curled over the edge of the tub's rim.

2

"IT'S THE FAULT of those ungrateful scum! Look at them out there on the grass. They don't want to work!"

The voice of the convalescent home's administrator trembled in outrage. Gustav Tanner was a diminutive man with a ferret face who was now intent on justifying the death to everyone present. Bea didn't like him. She mumbled a terse acknowledgment and turned toward the two nurses, an aide, and a doctor who hovered over the gurney where Fabian Bunting's body now rested.

"It's the strike," the administrator continued as he plucked Bea's sleeve. "They want the world handed to them on a platter. Look what happens. We're so shorthanded a patient was left unattended in the whirlpool. It's their fault. Out-and-out negligence that I blame on those outside agitators."

The portly doctor with muttonchop whiskers detached himself from the small group around the gurney and walked over to Bea and the administrator. "Cardiac arrest, Mr. Tanner." They all watched as a sheet was pulled over the face of Fabian Bunting, former doctor of philosophy and iconoclast.

"You'll put that on the certificate?"

"Of course."

The large male aide who had helped with the removal of the body caught Tanner's attention. "She was pretty unhappy here, Mr. Tanner. She could have done herself in."

Gustav Tanner considered this for a moment. Bea could imagine his mental machinations as he mulled over a fear of lawsuits and the reputation of the home and its staff.

"Patients have done it before."

"Crawled in a tub?" Bea asked.

The doctor closed his medical bag. "I'll complete my paper work in the office."

"Make sure it's cardiac arrest," Tanner yelled after the departing physician.

Bea felt Tanner's hand on her elbow as he attempted to steer her from the room. She turned to break his grip and walked over to the tub. The therapy bath rested on the floor on conical-shaped feet. A movable ladder seat could be wheeled to the edge where the occupant could either step into the tub or be lowered into the water. Bea noticed that the steps were in the far corner of the room. She felt the presence of the administrator by her side. "How did she get in, Mr. Tanner?"

"You may rest assured that I shall find out."

"And take appropriate action?"

"Naturally. And now, Mrs. . . ."

"Wentworth."

"My people would like to tidy up the room and make arrangements for Mrs. Bunting."

"Doctor Bunting."

"Of course."

Bea allowed herself to be led into the hallway. "Don't you find this odd, Mr. Tanner?"

"Odd? No, not really, Mrs. Wentworth. It must be shocking to you, but it is an unfortunate fact of life that we here in the home face death on a day-to-day basis."

"By scalding?"

"Cardiac arrest is commonplace in a woman of her age."

"Mr. Tanner, I found her. Remember?"

Tanner looked at her for a long moment. His eyes were cold and withdrawn. "Exactly what are you implying?"

"A fact."

"I assume you are suggesting that the patient made her way into the tub room by herself and . . ."

"I am not suggesting that at all."

"Since you were evidently her friend, if you would care to notify members of the family, please feel free to use the phone in the administration office." Tanner turned and walked back through the double doors.

The hall was deserted. Bea heard a low moan from a room down the hall. The nurses' station was vacant. She wondered whom to call. Fabian Bunting had outlived the members of her family and her past lovers. Only a small group of friends would mourn. Bea felt a tear on her cheek and brushed it away.

On impulse she went behind the counter of the station. A wheeled cart with several racks of charts hanging on their metal coverings was aligned against the wall. She searched until she found the one labeled Bunting. The day's entries were concise:

6:30 Patient awake. 7:00 Breakfast. 7:30 Meds.

The last entry. There wasn't any entry today or for the past week for physical therapy.

KIM AND BEA DRANK coffee in a narrow booth inside the Ice Cream Shoppe down the road from the convalescent home. Kim had taken Bea's arm when she left the home and had steered her toward the shop. The conversation concerning the strike had been animated and one-sided.

"They make minimum wage in there. My God, Bea, you know as well as I do that you can't live on one hundred thirty bucks a week and support a family. Most of them would be better off on welfare. At least then they'd be eligible for food stamps and free medical care. That fink Tanner comes back at us and says he can't give any raises without charging more to the patients—and that puts us in a real bind. Marty says that it's all a sweetheart deal. They have the money and can pay more. Are you listening? Bea?"

"What? Oh, sure, Kim."

"Lost interest in the working class?"

"No, of course not. Who's Marty?"

"Marty Rustman. He's the president of our local. A real fireball. One hell of a public speaker and quite a guy. A little flaky sometimes, but a real leader. Is something wrong?"

"Dr. Bunting is dead. It's taking me a little time to assimilate it. I'm sorry if I haven't paid attention."

"Fabian Bunting. That's too bad. She was quite a woman. It must have happened suddenly. We saw her leaning out the window yelling for us just before you arrived."

"Oh? What time was that?"

"It couldn't have been but a few minutes before you arrived. Then a little later I noticed her in the sun-room at the end of the second floor. She had a small pair of binoculars."

"Like opera glasses?"

"Yes. She watched us for a few minutes and then must have left, or else I didn't notice her."

"Minutes before I arrived?"

"I'm sure of it, because about that time we were hassling some scabs trying to cross the line."

"I think I had better make a call." She slid from the booth and crossed to a wall phone. She fumbled for a dime in the loose change in her pocketbook, dropped it in the slot, and held the humming receiver near her ear. Her index finger was poised over the dial. Lyon would be at work. He would be deeply immersed in his imaginary creatures as he hurried to complete the book for a Christmas publication date. His response would be vague and distant as he tried to shift mental gears and align himself with her fears. She made her decision and dialed the Murphysville Police Department. "Chief Herbert, please."

A connection was made quickly. "Herbert." The voice was deep and robust in keeping with the massive bulk of the man.

"Bea Wentworth, Rocco. There's been a death at the Murphysville Convalescent Home."

"Unfortunately there often is, Bea. It's hardly a police matter."

"Give me a moment." She quickly recounted her discovery of Dr. Bunting's body and the circumstances. She voiced her misgivings over the lack of chart notation and the time sequence between when Kim last saw the old lady and the approximate time of death.

"That hardly constitutes murder, Bea."

"The way things stand now, once the death certificate is signed, you won't even be involved, will you?"

"No reason to be. You know, they have a strike over there. Things are probably in a real mess, which might account for her being left unattended."

"I think it's more than that, Rocco."

"A motive of any sort?"

"I don't think so, but I'd still like you to come."

Rocco sighed. "All right, Bea. Give me a couple of minutes to tie up some loose ends."

He hung up and Bea stood by the phone for a few moments thinking about possible motives. Fabian Bunting had been a tenured professor at her alma mater. There was a husband somewhere back in the dim past, but Bea wasn't sure if the marriage had been dissolved in divorce or death; either way it must have been over thirty years ago. She didn't believe Fabian had a private income and assumed she probably subsisted on the modest pension the college provided. What possible motive could there be? Who would want to kill an eighty-four-year-old woman—irascible as she might have been sometimes?

Kim had paid for the coffee when Bea returned to the booth. They left the restaurant and walked back toward the picket line where Bea would wait for Rocco Herbert.

The van had stopped outside town where another man climbed into the cab. The man had glanced back toward the rear, where he was tied, and then they had driven on. He knew they were going to kill him. He was not particularly surprised. He had been threatened, beaten, and spat on before during his years of union organizing, and

16

this was not totally unexpected. He knew who they were and why they were doing it, but perhaps they would only beat him. A few blows with a baseball bat across the knees, a tire iron across the face, something that would hurt and maim but still allow him to survive. It was possible that he might live. He would hold on to that—it was all he had.

THE STRIKERS were clustered in groups. Their conversations erupted in angry buzzes, and Kim knew something was wrong. She left Bea and ran over to the first group. Her body shook with rage as she heard the accusations the nursing-home administrator had made. She turned to face Bea with her hands balled in tight fists.

"That bastard blames us."

"For what?"

"Dr. Bunting's death. He claims the noise of the strike upset her and caused her to become extremely agitated. Damn it, Bea! That woman was with us."

"What's wrong with that guy?" someone yelled.

"He says we're responsible."

"That's ridiculous."

"I know it, you know it, and he knows it. But that's the word that'll go out to the newspapers."

The police cruiser swerved to a halt in front of the home and was immediately surrounded by a score of strikers. Rocco Herbert unlimbered his mammoth body from the vehicle to face the gesticulating workers. He listened with his six-foot-eight height slouched toward a short Puerto Rican as the man's torrent of words shifted uncontrollably from Spanish to English. Rocco nodded, nodded again, and then turned away to walk toward Bea and Kim.

While watching the large man approach, Bea marveled, as she often did, at the close relationship between her husband and this massive police officer. They were such divergent individuals. Her husband was a quixotic and often dreamy man, while his friend, Rocco, was a pragmatic policeman who seemed constantly saddened by his perspective of the foibles of the human condition. Bea knew that the relationship had begun years ago when Rocco had served with Lyon in Korea. Her husband was a junior intelligence officer attached to Division G-2, while Rocco's Ranger company had been the eyes and ears that Lyon had so effectively utilized in his intelligence operations. The relationship had continued over the years, both men comfortable in each other's company, perhaps because their personalities complemented each other.

"Morning, Bea, Kim." Rocco touched the brim of his hat.

Bea took Rocco's arm and led him up the walk toward the main entrance of the nursing home. "Thanks for coming."

"You know how this is going to read out, Bea. The management is going to call you a troublemaker trying to make political points with the workers."

"When it comes to the murder of one of my friends, I'd like to make a hell of a lot of trouble."

"It's well known that Kim worked with you for years, and that now she's an organizer for the service workers. The allegation of impropriety by the home is going to seem like . . ."

"I don't operate that way, Rocco."

"I know. But I wonder if they do."

Gustav Tanner stood in the reception area nervously awaiting their arrival. His fingers moved with a life of their own, and his facial features seemed possessed by a slight tremor.

"I want those idiots moved away from here, Chief Herbert."

"Who might that be, Mr. Tanner?"

An extended finger pointed to the strikers clustered near the door. "Out there! That scum!"

"Have they broken the law?"

"They're disrupting routine."

"I believe that's their legal intention," Bea said.

"I'm here about the death of Dr. Bunting," Rocco said. "Can we talk in your office?"

IN TWENTY MINUTES Rocco had examined the death certificate and inspected the physical therapy room, where he paid close attention to the lethal tub. He requested Fabian Bunting's chart. The chart now lay open on the administrator's desk as his finger moved slowly down the entries. He read aloud: "Six-thirty, Patient awake. Seven, Breakfast. Seven-thirty, Meds. Nine-forty-five, Physical therapy. Ten-fifteen, Patient expired."

Bea gave a start and sat on the edge of her chair. "Read that again."

Rocco repeated the entries and then looked at her expectantly. "Well? Nothing unusual about the chart."

"That PT notation wasn't there when I looked at it earlier."

Tanner snapped the chart's metal cover shut and pulled it back across the desk. "Only authorized personnel are allowed to see a patient's medical records."

"That PT entry was not there when I left here."

"That's impossible."

"Do you know who made those last entries?" Rocco asked.

Tanner opened the chart and examined the handwriting carefully. "Miss Williams made the first three. I made the final notation. I can't tell who made the PT note. We're all off schedule here because of the strike."

"All right," Rocco said. "Let's find out who took Fabian Bunting to the tub room and made that entry."

THERE WERE TEN EMPLOYEES assigned to the second floor during the time span when Dr. Bunting died. They were a mixed group of administrative personnel, supervisors, two R.N.s, and an aide or two who chose to ignore the picket line and come to work. Most were quickly eliminated because they had been seen by others or were in other parts of the building during the thirty minutes when the scalding death would have had to occur. Four had taken a coffee break together and were in the canteen room during the crucial time period.

Bambi Williams, R.N., sat primly before the desk that was now occupied by Rocco. She clasped her hands on her starched lap and looked intently at Rocco as if to discern some hidden meaning in his posture.

"Where were you between nine-forty-five and ten-fifteen, Miss Williams?"

"I was giving out midmorning meds."

"Anyone see you?"

"The patients, of course. At least the ones who can still think." There was a biting edge in her voice, a vehemence that chilled the room and made Bea immediately feel compassion for the helpless individuals served by this bitter woman.

"And you took Dr. Bunting to the tub room during that period?"

"No."

"In the rush of events you forgot about her." Rocco's voice was matter of fact and without any judgmental quality.

"I certainly did not."

"Someone charted her for PT. The charts were in your possession during that period."

"They were at the nurses' station and available to anyone while I was in the rooms."

"Did you see anyone take Dr. Bunting to the tub room?"

"No. The last time I saw her she was careening down the hallway to the sun-room to make more trouble."

"What sort of trouble?" Bea interjected.

"She'd been yelling out her window all morning. I had to restrain her."

"Restrain?"

"Not in the physical sense. I took her away from the window and locked it. That's when she went to the sun-room and that's the last I saw of her."

"Thank you, Miss Williams."

The nurse rose from her chair as if catapulted and walked briskly toward the door.

"You didn't care for her, did you?" Bea said.

"She was a crotchety old bitch," Bambi Williams said as she left the room.

"I have the feeling that the lady does not like her work," Rocco said.

"God help the infirm. Who's next?"

Rocco looked down at his list. "The last one is an aide named Mike Maginacolda." He called out, "Mr. Maginacolda, please."

Maginacolda swaggered into the room. It took Bea a few moments to decipher what it was that made him incongruous in this setting. His defiant attitude initially put her off, but then she realized that it was his hospital whites. They fit too well. The usual bunch of fabric across the rear of the shoulders so usual in rented linens was missing. His uniform had been tailored.

Maginacolda slouched into the chair Rocco indicated. He glanced over at Bea with a smile of prurient, crude sexuality.

Rocco looked studiously at a personnel file in front of him. "It has been brought to our attention that you took Bunting to the physical therapy room."

"That's a goddamn lie!" Maginacolda leaned over the desk and slapped his palms loudly on its surface. "I was nowhere near the second floor when she croaked."

"Is that right?" Rocco looked impassively at the man bent over the desk. "Exactly where were you?"

The questioning continued as Rocco quietly probed at the angry aide. It seemed to go nowhere, and Bea realized it was fruitless. If anyone in the hospital had taken Fabian Bunting to PT, they were not admitting it—to anyone.

When Maginacolda started for the door, she asked him, "Why aren't you out on strike?"

"Hell, I'm shop steward for the bona fide local."

"I don't understand."

"My union always used to represent the workers here until Rustman and that black chick carded everyone and called an election. They'll wise up and we'll be back in the saddle soon."

"I see."

The aide left the room and Rocco shrugged as he closed the last file.

THE WENTWORTH HOME, Nutmeg Hill, was perched on a promontory overlooking the Connecticut River on the outskirts of Murphysville. Stands of pine surrounded the house on three sides and were parted by a long, winding drive that meandered up from the highway. A fieldstone patio at the rear of the house overlooked the river and was surrounded by a profusion of carefully tended spring flowers. Lyon and Bea had discovered the run-down house several years ago while hiking in the woods. They had purchased the decrepit dwelling and restored it with tender love. The old house's casual mixture of early American and contemporary furnishings enhanced the comfortable aura.

A large window in Lyon's study above the patio gave the impression that his desk floated above the river. Banks of bookcases and large, worn leather chairs completed the furnishings in his workroom.

Lyon was oblivious of the view as he hunched over the typewriter by the window.

He wasn't there.

He walked with his Wobblies. His monsters had made their way to a wooded place and now sat before a mountain stream to rest. The long tongues of his two friends lolled from the sides of their faces as they looked toward their creator with lopsided grins. Their enemy had been defeated. The Waldoons had once again been sent into exile from which they would undoubtedly return in the next book—it was a time of peace, a time of renewal; and yet the Wobblies were elated, and Lyon viewed them with satisfaction.

The tiny knock on the door dispelled the quiet. Lyon turned from the typewriter as his eyes refocused and he returned to reality.

"Who?"

"A very depressed lady." Bea stepped into the room and slumped into a leather chair. "The day started off lousy and has gone downhill since."

"Woeful Bea."

"KNOCK IT OFF, WENTWORTH."

"Your hearing aid battery is low again."

Bea fumbled in her ear for the small device, turned the volume up, and reinserted the instrument. "I wish I hadn't heard a word all day."

22

"That sounds like a riddle."

"I'm sorry to interrupt your work, but I would like you to hear what happened." She had put her thoughts in order on the drive home and now presented them in a clear and concise manner. As she talked, Lyon from time to time asked a quiet question or nodded. His frown deepened.

He gave a sigh when she finished. "What's Rocco going to do next?"

"He's ordered an autopsy over the nursing home's objections. We expect that it will show cardiac arrest due to the scalding. He's a little unsure as to what step to take next. There isn't any definite reason to believe that it's murder, but what bothers me is that no one will admit putting her into the tub. Also, what about the missing chart entry that so mysteriously appeared later?"

"A careless aide or nurse could be covering up for his or her own protection. A shorthanded staff, a forgotten patient . . . negligent but not malicious."

"Possibly, except a few minutes before she was killed, Kim saw Dr. Bunting in the sun-room holding opera glasses."

"And a nurse or aide came and took her to PT. He or she put her into the tub and left on another errand."

"You're making me feel paranoid."

"I don't mean to. I'm just considering other possibilities. There is one other answer."

"What's that?"

"Bunting herself."

"Suicide?"

"It's not uncommon with some older persons."

"Come on, Lyon. You met her. You know the woman's vitality and her zest."

"If she were afraid of losing her faculties . . . that could be devastating for such a person."

"But by scalding? What a painful way. If Fabian Bunting wanted to do herself in, I can see her finding a way to get into the medicine cabinet, but not into a hot tub."

Lyon tried to make the mental shift from his recent total involvement with his monsters to the possibility of a senseless death. For senseless is what it was. An old lady, without assets or heirs, obviously harmless to the world, had possibly been murdered.

"Anybody home?" Kim called from the vestibule.

"In the Lyon's den," Bea replied without moving.

"Oh, funny, funny." Kim entered the room pushing the bar cart. "It is cocktail time, right?"

"You know it," Bea said and began to mix martinis while Kim poured Lyon a pony of Dry Sack sherry. "A nice day on the barricades, hon?"

Kim sipped her martini and sat down. "Would have been. Could have been. We were to begin a negotiating session with management this afternoon, but fearless leader took off somewhere."

"I thought this . . . what's his name?"

"Rustman. Marty Rustman."

"Was the Sir Galahad of the labor movement."

"He's honest, militant, articulate, and flaky. Although I can't understand why he just disappeared."

Lyon turned his back on the panorama of the river. "Disappeared?"

"He was there at the home bright and early this morning when we set up the line. Sometime around ten this morning he took off. Funny thing about it is that he left his car."

Lyon leaned forward. "Are you sure it was ten?"

"Sometime around then. Why?"

"Did you call his office, the union headquarters, and so forth?"

"Damn right I did! I was fit to be tied. We had to cancel the meeting. You know, those workers really need the money—they need to work desperately."

"What about his home?"

Kim went to the telephone and dialed. It was answered on the first ring. "Mrs. Rustman? Kim Ward here. Is Marty there? . . . No. He left Murphysville about ten this morning and he's not at the union hall. . . . Have you heard from him? . . . No . . . Thank you." She slowly hung up: "Okay, what's coming down?"

24

"I wonder if there isn't a connection between Bunting's death and Marty Rustman's inexplicable disappearance."

"She was last seen in the sun-room with opera glasses," Bea said.

"If there's no sign of him in the morning, I think we had better talk to Rocco," Lyon said.

The van stopped after jouncing over several miles of dirt road. The rear doors were thrown open and he was pulled unceremoniously from the rear compartment and thrown onto the ground. He tried to mumble through the tape across his mouth, but the two men standing by the side of the van didn't look his way. After a few moments of consultation, one of them took a shovel from the rear of the van and walked twenty yards into the woods along the side of the logging road. He watched in fascination as the man inspected the ground carefully and then stuck the shovel into the earth. The man gave a grunt as the shovel cut through the layer of forest carpet and topsoil. He put the first shovelful of earth neatly to the side. They were going to kill him. There would be no baseball bat that would allow him to live another day. They were going to bury him!

3

THE RUSTMAN HOME was a small, white ranch with dark blue shutters located in the south end of Hartford. Bea turned the Datsun into the driveway and sat for a moment looking at the house. The grass was newly mown, the yard neat, and to the rear she could see an above-ground swimming pool where two tow-headed children played. The boy appeared to be around ten, the girl perhaps eight. They laughed with that distinctive sound children make when playing in water.

She had been elected for the trip by default. Right after breakfast Lyon had run for the safety of his study. Kim had phoned from the picket line and said that Marty Rustman had never arrived.

She left the car and went up the narrow cement walk to the front door and rang the bell. The door was opened immediately by a thirtyish woman with washed-out blond hair that hung in stray wisps across her forehead. Her face was haggard with deep pockets of worry under each eye. She uttered a tentative "Yes?"

"I'm Bea Wentworth, Mrs. Rustman. Kim Ward who works with your husband asked that I stop by."

"You know something about Marty?"

"That's why I'm here. To find out where he is."

"Oh. Please come in."

Bea followed Barbara Rustman through the living room into a

sun-drenched kitchen. Being a haphazard housekeeper herself, she immediately recognized in their brief journey the signs of the obsessive cleaner and scrubber. She sat at a small kitchen table while Barbara Rustman prepared coffee. There was a haunted quality to the woman standing at the stove. She carried a deep burden and had for more than the few hours her husband had been missing. It was a deeply ingrained hurt that had been lived with for years, and was probably only alleviated by constant work.

Barbara Rustman placed a coffee cup before Bea and sat across the table. "I don't know where Marty is, Senator Wentworth."

Bea laughed. "Not senator anymore. In fact, I'm temporarily out of politics."

"Marty always admired you and agreed with your stands."

"It's too bad you're not in my voting district. Kim Ward tells me only good things about your husband. She feels that he's a real asset to the labor movement."

"Let me show you the article in *Time* magazine." She reached into a kitchen drawer and placed a neatly clipped article before Bea.

Bea read the article. It praised Marty as one of the new breed of young labor leaders. At a recent national convention he had given an impromptu speech from the floor and received a standing ovation. The end of the article recounted his background. He had served in Vietnam as a medical corpsman and upon discharge had obtained a job as a lab technician at a Hartford hospital. When a union received NLRB sanction to hold an election at the hospital, Rustman had attended the organizational meeting. During the proceedings he had been elected shop steward. In a year's time he had become disenchanted with the union and resigned in protest. He formed an independent local, and in the space of a few years his union had won election after election, which forced management recognition. Recently his locals had been admitted into the AFL-CIO.

She looked up at Barbara sitting expectantly across the table. "He sounds like quite a guy."

"Does anyone know where he is?"

"We thought you could help."

"I don't know what to say. He's stayed away before at night. All-night negotiations and things like that, but he always called and told me where he was. He made a point of speaking to the children before they went to bed."

A child's laugh from the rear yard penetrated the room and Barbara Rustman seemed to cringe away from the sound. Bea realized that the woman was a permanent victim, drained and immersed in expected hurt. A woman whose vital forces had been sucked from her until she was a hollow receptacle awaiting further pain. A victim not of a specific battle but of the constant skirmishs that shaped her life.

The truth about Marty Rustman did not lie in the mechanical pride his wife exhibited. It rested within the province of the quiet moments husband and wife spent together.

"I'm so worried about Marty."

The same repetitive phrase. "Did you call the police?" Bea asked brusquely.

"The police? Of course not."

"Why not?"

"Well . . . I . . . He might come home any minute."

Out of shame for what she was going to do, Bea closed her eyes briefly. In that moment, as if she could hear the vital voice of Fabian Bunting, she knew she must find out the truth. She knew that she could break this emotionally frail woman sitting before her. The buttons were there, waiting to be pushed.

"He's with a slut again," Bea said harshly as she knotted her fingers into fists under the table.

There was a sharp intake of breath from the woman across the table. Words faltered and stumbled. "No . . . He wouldn't do . . . I don't know."

"He did last time."

"That was different. He'd won an election, he'd been drinking."

"And you think he's off whoring now. Don't you!" Bea leaned across the table and closed her hands over the other woman's clenched fingers.

"Yes. Yes. Yes."

Bea sat back slowly in her chair as Barbara Rustman's eyes clouded and feeling retreated to some inner place. She asked softly, "Want to talk about it?"

"There's no one to listen."

Her voice softer still. "I will."

The words began like a small freshet trickling down from a craggy ledge. They picked up strength as they tumbled into a rushing mountain stream, becoming a torrent of words that spilled over each other in their rush for expression. Bea listened without comment and felt the hurt.

"We grew up together. Not ten blocks from here. We lived next door to each other. Everyone always said we were meant for each other. I never dated anyone else. I think Marty did once in a while on the sly, but he always came back to me. We went to all the high school dances together and then got married a week after we graduated. It was wonderful in those days."

Bea nodded, although it wasn't necessary.

"I got a job right off, filing at the insurance company, and we had this great little apartment in a three-family house. Marty was always ambitious and didn't want to work in the aircraft like his dad. He went to technical school. A good lab tech can always get a job. After the two-year course, he got a job at the hospital. Then he went to Vietnam. . . ."

"That changed a lot of men."

The other woman looked at Bea as if the simplistic statement was a unique revelation. "Yes. Changed. He changed. He was one of those medical guys that went with the soldiers."

"A corpsman."

"When he came back, he was different. When we made . . . when he went to bed with me, it was different. He seemed to want to hurt me. I knew he was unhappy back at the hospital. Then when he got involved with the union, it seemed as if he liked the battles and arguments. He liked the organizing, the yelling, the picket lines, and sometimes the fights."

"Did anyone ever threaten him?"

29

"All the time. It used to frighten us, but we got used to it. They'd call up in the middle of the night and say they were waiting for him . . . things like that."

"Anyone specific?"

"It had gotten worse recently. There were a lot of problems at the convalescent homes. Marty said there was a sweetheart deal between union and management in several of the homes. He said they were corrupt and ought to be exposed. He liked a fight like that. In Murphysville he had to take on the old union and management at the same time. After he won a fight, he'd go off and have a few drinks someplace and then maybe a few more and go off with . . . it was never the same."

The tears had been held within her for a long time, and when they brimmed her eyes, she seemed to melt. Her body shook violently in an arch of grief, and Bea comforted her.

They pulled him along the ground. His head hit rocks and roots as it bumped along the forest floor. They dragged him to the grave and dropped him in. His face hit the bottom. His eyes were wide as they stared at the rich loam inches from his face. He knew he was a dead man.

The shot seared the rear of his skull. He felt a ring of blood seep over his forehead and into his eyes. The sun was warm. His body convulsed as the first shovelful of dirt fell onto the small of his back . . . and then more . . . and more . . . as they buried him.

ROCCO RETREATED into the small room he had built near the boiler in the cellar of his home. Martha and Remley were in Boston for the weekend, which made the night his. He pulled a paint-splattered kitchen chair across the rough cement floor and centered it carefully in front of the doll house. A pint of vodka lay in the workbench drawer. He flipped off the top and poured a jelly glass half full. He held the glass casually and tilted his chair back while he looked into the serenity of the miniature Victorian mansion.

It had been a bad day. A lot of them were. The kid had been picked up after running a stop sign and was found to be driving with a suspended license. Jamie Martin had brought him in for booking after confiscating an ounce of grass. Rocco had passed through the processing room when the kid had lunged for him. The roundhouse blow had glanced off his right cheek and barely staggered him.

He had reacted automatically. His fingers had extended into a straight plane as his hand swung forward in a blow that caught the kid across the larynx. He had stood over the prone body as his victim gasped for breath. His long arms had hung loosely by his side with the fingers balled into fists. When it was apparent that the kid writhing on the floor had not suffered permanent damage, he had left the room without a word.

It was such incidents that made them call him a mean son of a bitch. It was always the young ones between seventeen and twenty-five who caused the problems. Over the years he had become, he suspected, brutalized by them to the point where he reacted without thought, as he had this afternoon.

He needed this quiet time, this serenity before his miniatures. He drank vodka and considered rearranging the living room. He carefully placed the glass back on the workbench and began to move furniture in the front parlor. It was an ordered place, a place without mayhem, where young men wore black suits with high Celluloid collars, went to work each morning, and courted girls on veranda swings before the diffused illumination of gas lamps.

"What you need is a Victrola. One of those little ones with a speaker horn and the listening dog."

"If you wore shoes instead of those ridiculous half-assed sneakers, I would have heard you coming. The sherry's in the paint cabinet behind the gallon of gloss."

"Martha must be away," Lyon said as he extracted a bottle of wine and poured some into a second jelly glass.

"Boston. Do you think the sofa should go along this wall?" He made a minor adjustment to a four-inch-long divan.

"Probably. What are you doing about Fabian Bunting?"

"Turned what I had over to the state prosecutor, who promptly shipped it back. He thinks I'm nuts. People do die in convalescent homes, and this is the third scalding death we've had in the state this year."

"Rustman's still missing."

"Bea called me about that. He's probably holed up in some motel with a broad."

"Kim says no. He would never do that in the midst of a strike."

"How do you read it?" Rocco moved the bureau in the master bedroom.

"She saw someone kidnap Rustman and they disposed of her."

"I called Pasquale in Hartford. The wife hasn't filed a missing persons yet."

"I think you had better start looking for him. I have the feeling that if we find who took Rustman, we'll know who killed Fabian Bunting."

"Back to square one—find Rustman."

"You should."

At NUTMEG HILL Lyon trundled the folded envelope out from the barn on a two-wheeled cart and began to spread out the hot-air balloon on the grass. It would probably be circumspect to wait until Bea returned home so that she could follow him in the chase truck, but he was impatient to be aloft. He would phone her when he landed.

When the envelope was extended its full length, he started the small compressor to drive air into the bag. When the balloon began to billow and the aperture was wide enough, he held the propane burner across his waist and lit the pilot light. The jutting flame whooshed to life and began to heat the air inside the balloon.

In minutes the balloon began to rise slowly from the ground until it bounced overhead. He attached the burner to the ring above the gondola and then gave the flame a few seconds of burn until the balloon stabilized. He made preflight checks and untied the safety line tethered to the large oak. One last burn and the balloon shot upward.

There was a slight wind from the northeast that would push the large balloon past the green over Murphysville. If his calculations were correct, he would eventually pass over the convalescent home.

He leaned over the edge of the wicker basket with his arms folded. A panorama of his life was spread out below. A few miles up the river was Middleburg College where he had taught until suddenly realizing one morning that he was able to support his family from the royalties of his children's books. Now the balloon was over the green. Below was police headquarters; two blocks to the right, near the steepled Congregational Church, was the house where he and Bea had once lived—until their little girl was struck down while riding her first bicycle. They had left the house that very day and never returned.

He shook his head to dispel the thoughts. The balloon was drifting slowly past the convalescent home. A thin line of pickets, fewer in number than yesterday, meandered down the home's front walk. His interest was held by the north side of the building where below the sun-room there was a walled courtyard enclosed on three sides. A dumpster was parked to one side of a loading platform. Any vehicle in the courtyard would be well hidden from the view of those on the line in front of the home. In fact, it might not be seen by anyone except an old lady at the sun-room window with an ancient pair of opera glasses.

That's how it had been. A car, truck, or perhaps a van had been parked in the enclosure. Rustman was thrust inside and driven away. Which way did they go? A turn to the left would take the vehicle toward the green and the most populous part of town. If it turned right, it would pass few homes until it was in the country.

The wind pushed the balloon past the home. He wondered if his aerial path was following the same direction as that taken by the vehicle bearing Rustman.

He was convinced that Rustman had been taken involuntarily from the home and that Fabian Bunting had seen the abduction. He had faith in Kim's assessment that Marty would never have left the area voluntarily when an important negotiating session was imminent. The question now was, What had they done with him?

33

The balloon reached the outskirts of town and began to pass over an undeveloped state forest. It was a dense area filled with heavy undergrowth and only utilized by hunters during the season. It was crisscrossed by old logging roads and a labyrinth of wooded coves and isolated cul-de-sacs.

Finding Rustman would be nearly an impossible task. In addition to the hundreds of acres of state forest, there was the nearby Connecticut River. He had known it to happen before—a week, month, or years from now a group of Boy Scouts might come across a shallow grave whose covering had been disturbed by predators. Or a fisherman on the river might snag a perforated oil drum made light by the buildup of internal gases from a decomposing body. Or Rustman might never be found.

It was time to pick a place to land, and he began to survey the ground below intently. The winding river to the right was flanked on each side by high bluffs. Most of the land below was woods, and directly ahead was the high stack of the Crown Point nuclear energy plant. His altitude was now dangerously low and his forward direction was neatly aligned with the top of the spewing smokestack.

Lyon knew that the stack released superheated steam into the atmosphere. If the balloon passed too close, the effect of the steam on the interior of the balloon envelope would be disastrous. There was no mechanism to steer the balloon, and the tall stack with its white column of steam was too high for the balloon to pass over, even with an additional propane burn.

He yanked the ripping panel. Huge gusts of hot air spilled from the open side of the envelope, and the balloon began a rapid descent. He calculated touchdown as safely forward of the reactor building and within the confines of the chain link fence that surrounded the facility.

As his rate of descent increased, he put on a crash helmet and gave the burner a few quick bursts of propane to slow the speed of his fall. When he was fifty feet from the ground, a siren wailed and uniformed men rushed from the gatehouse toward the main building. The balloon basket landed with a thump that tumbled Lyon over the side.

He shook his head groggily. As his eyes began to focus, he found himself facing the barrels of four M-16s held at the ready by grim-faced men.

"It's customary to share a bottle of champagne at an unexpected landing," Lyon said as four rifle bolts clicked four rounds into four chambers.

"IF THE FIRST SELECTMAN sees this, my next year's budget is zip." Rocco Herbert grimly drove the police cruiser back to Murphysville. The back of the car was stuffed with the rolled balloon envelope, while the wicker gondola was roped to the top.

"Those security guards don't have much sense of humor."

"Who would when some idiot falls out of the sky in a vehicle that looks like it came from another century?"

"You're going to book me?"

"As far as those security guards are concerned, you're arrested for trespassing, unauthorized flight, and reckless endangerment."

"But released on my own recognizance."

"I'd like to put that balloon in storage as evidence forever. Did you find out anything?"

"That we're probably never going to find Rustman's body."

"You're positive it's out there somewhere?"

"I think so. I think we'll have to approach things from a different angle. Perhaps some more information at the nursing home."

"Bea is persona non grata out there."

"She'll find a way. Have you turned up anything else?"

"Two of the strikers think they saw a red van drive from the courtyard of the nursing home about ten that morning. No one remembers who was in it or the license plate number."

"That figures."

THE MURPHYSVILLE CAPELLA CANTORUM was composed of thirty-five men and women of diverse backgrounds. They were businessmen and women, machinists, a professor or two from Middleburg College, and housewives. They met every Tuesday night for one purpose—to sing. They had made arrangements to give a lunch-hour concert to the inhabitants of the Murphysville Convalescent Home. Bea followed them in the pickup truck. She parked at the rear of the entourage as they assembled in front of the home.

While following the singers into the building, she noticed that the ranks of the strikers had noticeably thinned out. Kim marched resolutely with a picket sign, but only two other workers were present. The black woman looked her way and raised an eyebrow when Bea failed to respond. Kim nodded in understanding and marched in the other direction.

Inside the home Bea saw Dale Winters, the conductor of the group, talking with the administrator. Tanner directed the choir down the hall toward the recreation room on the first floor.

Marcia Dabner, who owned the Murphysville Pharmacy, fell in step with Bea. "I thought you tried out for the choir in sixty-five, Beatrice?"

"I did. As I recall, I was unanimously not accepted."

"You've improved?"

"Nope."

"Worse?"

"Probably."

"Lord help us."

"Just visiting. I promise not to spoil your concert."

Bea peeled off from the herd of singers and entered the elevator. She simultaneously pushed the button for the second floor and the "close door" button. All the ambulatory patients and those who could sit comfortably in wheelchairs would be at the concert, as would most of the remaining help. The elevator door opened on the second floor. The nurses' station was vacant. She strode rapidly down the hall toward the PT room and she pushed through the doors.

The galvanized tub looked anything but ominous. She moved the small ladder stool toward the tub in which Bunting had died. She stepped up the ladder, let her feet dangle over the edge, and then jumped lightly into the empty tub. It was chest high, and she tried to imagine the buoyancy she would feel if it were filled with water. The hot and cold faucets were at the far side of the tub placed on the intake pipes near a temperature gauge that was three-quarters of the way down the side of the tub. She stood near the pipes and leaned over. Her fingers were barely able to brush the spigot handle. It seemed unlikely that the five-foot-two-inch Fabian Bunting would be physically capable of turning on the faucets from inside the tub. She discounted the possibility that her old teacher had adjusted the water from outside the tub and then crawled inside. The woman had just undergone a hip operation and had been confined to a wheelchair.

The evidence seemed more conclusive than ever that Bunting had been placed in the tub and then the scalding water had been turned on.

Bea climbed out of the tub and was about to push through the swinging doors when she noticed the two men.

Gustav Tanner was sitting on the edge of the station counter with his legs dangling off the side. Maginacolda leaned against the wall with the same insolent look that Bea had observed in the office during Rocco's interview. There was an intimacy between the two men. Maginacolda was speaking while Tanner seemed to be listening with great interest.

Tanner looked out of character. He always assumed the mantle of the irate manager and officious administrator. Casual banter with an aide seemed wrong, particularly when it was an employee who had once been a union steward.

Maginacolda noticed her. He jerked away from the wall, rushed toward the PT room doors, and pulled her into the hall. "What in hell are you doing here?"

"Looking for the ladies room." He pushed her against the wall. "Hey!"

Tanner trembled in rage. "Who let you in?"

"I walked through the front door."

The two men exchanged a quick look. Tanner shook his head. "Just get her out of here and don't let her back in!"

37

She was firmly escorted to the main entrance. Before the front door swung shut, Maginacolda grasped her arm painfully. "I wouldn't come back. Understand?"

Bea walked to her truck. She would tell Lyon what she had observed, but the physical abuse might better be left unsaid.

AFTERWARD WAS NEARLY her favorite time. They lay flank to flank. A soft peace filled the bedroom as she nuzzled against Lyon's shoulder. His hand brushed lightly along her neck and she knew he was still awake.

"Thinking?"

"In a lazy way. I can't figure out what's going on at the nursing home."

"You worry about finishing your book. I'll think about Tanner and the other one." She sighed. "At least I'll think about it in the morning."

He reached across in the dim light and picked up her bare arm and looked at the black-and-blue marks on her bicep. "What happened to you?"

She looked at the bruise that Maginacolda had made. "Oh, I don't know," she lied. "I must have fallen against something."

"Bea?"

The shrill ring of the phone saved her. He reached for the receiver on the bedside table. "Uh huh . . . Right . . . Rocco, do you think it might be Rustman? . . . Yes, I'll come and bring Kim to make the ID. . . . No, that's all right." He hung up and slid from the bed.

"They've found the body?"

"All my fancy theories and balloon trip wasted. The body's behind the convalescent home."

"You want me to come?"

"No, get some sleep. It's after midnight."

"I won't be able to sleep a wink until you get back," she said, and was asleep before his car left the driveway.

4

A DEAD WRIST with limp fingers was draped over the edge of the wooden concrete form like fingers trailing the water from a slowly drifting canoe.

The construction site at the rear of the Murphysville Convalescent Home was partially illuminated by the headlights of three police cruisers. Lyon parked the pickup next to car MU-1 and stepped over beams and sand toward a wooden frame where Rocco stood.

Rocco glanced at him and then pointed to the concrete form filled with hardening cement where the hand dangled.

"How was it found?"

"Couple of aides on the midnight shift came out here for a smoke."

The assistant medical examiner scowled down at his muddy shoes as he picked his way across the construction site toward them. His frown deepened when he saw the protruding hand. "Oh, Christ. This one's going to be a mess."

"We were waiting for you before we pulled it out, doc."

An ambulance backed toward the concrete form and two attendants unrolled a body bag and stood waiting by a stretcher. Rocco signaled to two patrolmen who cautiously approached the hardening concrete. They stepped into the form. The mixture slurped up the sides of their hip boots. With a mutual nod they reached down and struggled to free the body from the cement. The corpse, covered in oozing white, slowly emerged, and they rolled it onto the body bag.

The medical examiner stooped near the corpse and swabbed some cement from the face. His hand gently brushed the windpipe and then he pried open the jaws and peered into the interior of the mouth cavity with a penlight.

"Probable death by gross asphyxiation. I'd take a rough guess at time of death as within the last two to three hours. I'll get you more precise info when I've had it on the table."

"Good Lord!" Tanner stepped toward the body. It was obvious that he had dressed quickly as striped pajama bottoms stuck out below his pants. "It's Mike."

Rocco turned in surprise. "It's not Marty Rustman?"

"Of course not. Its Mike Maginacolda. He's still got on his hospital whites. Rustman and Mike don't look anything alike."

"It sure isn't Rustman," Kim said from Lyon's side.

"Oh, Christ! This I don't need," Rocco said. He vented his anger by yelling at the surrounding police. "All right! Don't stand around like dummies. You know what to do."

Lyon and Kim retreated to the periphery of activity as a large searchlight was brought to the site. A portable generator coughed to life and the area was immediately bathed in glaring light. Rocco gave directions for a minute search of the area as a photographer completed pictures.

Kim shook her head as Lyon turned the key in the ignition of the pickup. "I don't understand what's going on here."

"What was the relationship between Rustman and Maginacolda?"

"That's what's so damn strange. They hated each other. You have to understand that they were really enemies. Maginacolda was steward for the other union, a cruddy outfit that everybody knew had sweetheart contracts with management."

"Which Rustman was trying to break?"

"Which he was breaking. We were winning the strike, Lyon. And we had already won the election for representation. It was a question of time until . . . that was when Marty disappeared. Now, more than half my people have gone back to work."

"I can't imagine how kidnapping Rustman in order to break one strike at a relatively small convalescent home would be justified in anyone's mind."

"It wasn't just Murphysville. This was Marty's first attack against the Shopton Corporation. They own a whole series of homes plus other businesses. Each one has the same union deal."

"That certainly gives Rustman's disappearance more significance."

SHE HATED THEM.

As she stood before them she felt irrational, hating a living thing with such fervor. She had tried poison—iron sulphate in a mixture of two pounds to a gallon of water, but still they flourished.

Bea Wentworth hated ignorance, people with closed minds, and weeds. On this particular morning she thought she might even reverse that order. The Japanese honeysuckle, a rampant vine with dingy white flowers, had captured the side of the parapet wall on the patio. Every solution she applied seemed to increase rather than hinder their growth. Four weeks ago she had pulled them by hand, back- and knee-breaking work that seemed to propagate them further.

"Somehow you're going to get it," she said aloud. She sat cross-legged on the patio and examined her enemies. Intruder weeds, particularly the Japanese honeysuckle, should be burned out. She wondered if the governor would arrange for her to borrow a flame-thrower from the National Guard. Dunbar's Hardware probably sold a small garden unit, but her innate New England frugality made her hesitate to spend the money. There must be another way.

She could hear Lyon's typewriter in the study and knew that he was nearly finished with the book. Lyon . . . yes . . . his toy!

LYON SOMETIMES FELT that for a writer they were the two nicest words in the English language. He centered the typewriter carriage,

41

flipped the paper down six spaces, and typed them carefully: The End. He leaned over his machine, drained from weeks of emotional effort and all-consuming work.

The loud *whoosh* outside the study window made him reflexively push his desk chair back and retreat across the room. He knew what it was. When the *whoosh* was repeated, he saw flame spatter up toward the window. He dashed for the door.

A hot-air balloon only a few feet from the house was in distress. The accident might kill the operator. He hoped he could aid him before the wind caught the envelope and pushed it off the edge of the parapet and down the ridge into the water below.

He stopped in the patio doorway in amazement. Bea, dressed in a scanty halter and frayed shorts topped by a floppy hat, had his balloon propane tank in a wheelbarrow. She was balancing the burner against her waist as she aimed flame at the recalcitrant weeds growing along the parapet wall.

"Beatrice! That's overkill." She didn't seem to hear and flipped the lever for another burn. Lyon heard the phone in the kitchen and tumbled the receiver from its place on the wall.

He spoke briefly to Rocco and hung up. He picked up Bea's hearing aid from the kitchen counter and went out on the patio. He caught her attention and slid the small device into her ear. "Rocco just called. I think we had better go down to police headquarters."

She looked at the charred weeds. "You go. I have to finish these finks off."

"I think you had better come along. It's about Kim."

She looked at him in alarm. "Something's happened to her?"

"She's been arrested."

KIMBERLY WARD STOOD impassively before the camera as Jamie Martin adjusted the small sign hanging around her neck. White letters against a dark background spelled out her name, Murphysville P.D., and the date. Martin finished the adjustments and stepped back behind the camera.

Rocco slouched against the wall with arms akimbo observing the proceedings as Lyon and Bea came to the door.

"What's the charge?" Lyon asked.

"Assault."

Jamie Martin finished three sets of pictures and removed the sign from Kim. He began to fill out a form at a waist-high table. "Have you ever been arrested before, Mrs. Ward?"

Kim shrugged. "You want everything?"

"All prior arrests. We'll find out eventually from the FBI files."

"Thirty-two times."

The young officer looked startled and stopped writing. He glanced at Kim and then over to Rocco. "Thirty-two?"

"Get them all," Rocco said without smiling.

"The form's not long enough, sir."

"Use additional sheets."

Jamie Martin pulled a stool over to the table and sat down in a hunched position prepared for a long writing assignment. "Start from the earliest."

"1964, Selma, Alabama. Three times. I think they called it trespassing, or was there one trespassing and two unlawful assemblies?"

"I'll put trespassing."

"The Welfare Mothers' march in Hartford. That was in sixty-eight or was it sixty-seven?"

"Sixty-seven," Bea said.

Kim continued a recitation that seemed to cover every protest and civil rights march on the Eastern seaboard.

"Please tell us what's going on," Lyon said.

"You know, I have more to do than busting Kim. Somebody stole a damn dump truck from Wainwright Construction."

"Whom did she assault?"

"Mary Washington."

"She's one of the workers at the home, isn't she?"

"She's become a scab, not a worker," Kim replied as Jamie Martin began to roll her fingers on a fingerprint chart. "She broke the line and went to work."

"Kim slapped her," Rocco said with resignation.

"Twice," Martin added.

They finished the fingerprinting and the patrolman gave a powdered solution to Kim to cleanse her hands. "I shouldn't have hit her, but God, it's been a bad day. I think we're losing the strike. All that suffering, and we lost. To make matters worse, somebody broke into the union office and stole about three grand of ours."

"That's in Hartford, thank God," Rocco said. "Pat's got the case."

"Why do you keep so much cash around?"

"It was emergency strike money, all we had. We parceled it out to those who needed it the most. Marty kept it in cash hidden in the office."

"Any forced entry?" Lyon asked.

"No. They must have slipped the lock and knew right where the money was."

The uniformed officer had another form and looked at Rocco. "Own recognizance, Chief?"

Rocco nodded. "As long as Mrs. Ward promises not to pull an Angela Davis on us."

Kim glared. "And how come there aren't any brothers in your fascist gang, Chief?"

"Because the brothers who live in this town won't work for the lousy money we pay."

"I'll bet."

"Now damn it, Kim!"

Lyon took Rocco's arm and led him down the hall. "What about the investigation."

"We're going to Maginacolda's apartment this morning. I'm meeting Sergeant Pasquale over there in half an hour."

"Mind if I come?"

"Wish you would."

As they walked toward the parking lot and Rocco's car, Lyon saw Kim and Bea go out the front door. Jamie Martin leaned out of the processing room doorway to look at Bea's legs, which were still barely encased in skimpy shorts. Lyon didn't know whether to be pleased at his wife's figure or angry at the officer.

Rocco parked the cruiser in front of a high-rise apartment building in Hartford. He was approached immediately by a uniformed doorman who leaned in the driver's window. "Help you, officer?"

"Sergeant Pasquale here?"

"He's with the super getting a key to five-oh-eight."

"My friend and I will be going with him. Tell him we're here."

The doorman gave a two-fingered salute to the brim of his cap and picked up a phone in the vestibule. Lyon and Rocco went into the lobby to wait. Lyon walked across the marble tile to examine a statue in a corner lit by recessed spots. It was a modernistic figure chiseled from Vermont marble.

"You know what I'm wondering?" Rocco said behind him.

"Yep. How a nurse's aide making one hundred fifty dollars a week could afford to live in the 'Towers' where the apartments start at five hundred a month."

"Yeah, that too. But why would anyone steal a dump truck? Kids, I guess. Always the kids."

Detective Sergeant Pat Pasquale of the Hartford Police stepped out of the elevator. The short officer thumped Rocco on the shoulder. "Christ, you wop bastard! I think you're still growing."

"Rose let you out of the house this morning with your pop gun, Pat?"

The sergeant cocked his head. "I got to think about that one before I decide how insulted I am."

"You got the key to the Maginacolda place?"

"Let's go." They walked into the waiting elevator.

Apartment 508 had obviously been furnished by a decorator. The small vestibule, living room, kitchen, and bedroom were done completely in white and black. A massive curved sofa covered with a tufted white material rounded one wall. Casual pillows of black were strewn intermittently along its length. The carpet was white and the drapes black. Pasquale stepped into the bedroom and looked up at the ceiling where a large mirror was positioned directly over the bed. He whistled. "A goddamn French whorehouse."

Lyon sat on one of the steps that led down from the front door to

45

the living room. He leaned against a wrought-iron rail. The two police officers began a meticulous search of the apartment. With inflation, it would be difficult to make an estimate as to the cost of the apartment's furnishings, but the expense was considerable. Maginacolda lived well.

Rocco found two savings account passbooks and a checkbook in a table drawer. He rapidly flipped pages to check their last balances. "How much?" Lyon asked.

"Fourteen in one, nineteen in the second, and a balance brought forward in the checking account of five."

"Total assets of thirty-eight thousand."

"That we know of."

Pat came out of the bedroom with a .45 automatic held in a handkerchief. "Hey, look at this."

"Loaded?"

"Full clip."

"If you look near where you found that, you'll also find a pair of brass knuckles or a blackjack," Lyon said.

Pat looked at him sharply. "How do you know?"

"I have the feeling that Maginacolda was more than an aide and shop steward. He was probably involved in more than a little strong-arm work."

Rocco glanced around the apartment. "It must have paid well."

JASON SMELTS HID behind an unlit cigar and glared at the two police officers and Lyon seated before his desk. His salt-and-pepper hair was waved and styled, while the seersucker suit seemed almost a caricature of what the well-dressed union president should wear. The union headquarters was located in Hartford in a neat one-story building centered on a well-landscaped plot. Smelts's office was a large room with a broad mahogany desk, which was free of any work clutter, and a neat row of garishly upholstered side chairs, which were a testament to bad taste. Lyon wondered if Smelts and Maginacolda shared the same decorator.

Smelts waved the cigar like a brandished cutlass. "Find Rustman and you've got the guy who blew Maginacolda away."

Pat flipped a pad from his sport jacket pocket. "Exactly what were your dealings with Mr. Maginacolda, Mr. Smelts?"

"Friend and advisor."

"When was the last time you saw him?"

"Week ago. He came in here right after he lost the election with Rustman."

"Did he say anything that might make you think he was fearful for his life?"

"Yeah. He said that Rustman was real trouble. Not that that fact was news here."

"How's that?"

"Ever since Rustman broke away from this union and formed his own, he's been attacking our locals whenever he gets a chance."

"By attacking, what do you mean?"

"Trying to get control."

"Through NLRB elections," Lyon said.

"Same difference. Who's he?" The cigar made a rapierlike thrust toward Lyon.

"Wentworth's from Murphysville," Rocco said with an unspoken implication that Lyon served on the force.

"Did Maginacolda receive any salary or fees from the union?" Pat asked.

The cigar was thrust in the mouth. "That's union business."

"It's police business now," Rocco said.

"I can have a court order in thirty minutes," Pat said.

Jason Smelts shrugged. "A little here, a little there. Mike was what we call one of our troubleshooters. You can't expect a guy to do that without a little extra on the side."

"How much is a little?"

The shoulders shrugged and the cigar waved expansively. "I'd have to ask the bookkeeper. Come back in four or five . . ."

"A ball-park figure," Rocco said in a tone that Lyon had heard so often in past interrogation sessions.

"Forty or fifty. Somewhere in that area."

"Forty what and how often?"

"Thou a year."

"I was led to believe that he was a shop steward at the Murphysville home," Lyon said. "In that case, he would have been elected by the workers there."

"What do the rank and file know? When we get a small shop not big enough for a full-time BA, we put our own man in there to get things going. We put out the word we want him elected."

"BA?"

"Business agent. A paid member like me."

"You transferred Maginacolda from one shop to another—when you needed him?"

"That's right. And when Rustman attacked in Murphysville, I put my best man in there—Mike."

"Doesn't sound very democratic."

"When Rustman came after us, we fought fire with fire."

"Can you be more explicit about that?"

"Huh?"

"Exactly how did you combat Rustman's union?"

"Well, hell! The usual ways. We talk to the rank and file, hold elections, work through the NLRB, the usual."

"And lean a little on people?"

"Them's your words, not mine." Jason Smelts leaned back in his chair and observed them warily through a protective haze of cigar smoke.

"Are you affiliated with the AFL-CIO?" Lyon asked.

"We're an independent."

"Where are your members located?"

"We got members in a couple dozen nursing homes, five hospitals, maintenance workers in about fifty buildings, a few places like that. We're still growing."

Pasquale flipped the pages of his pad and cleared his throat. "Mr. Smelts, since Maginacolda was involved in . . ." The detective fumbled for delicate wording. "Strong-arm tactics."

"I didn't say that. He was a trained representative in personal persuasion."

"In his attempts at persuasion, is it possible that he developed enemies?"

Smelts shrugged and stubbed out the cigar. "You can't make an omelet without breaking eggs."

Or heads, Lyon thought. He didn't care for the tone and aura that seemed to surround this union and could understand why Kim and Rustman were so bitterly opposed to its existence. If Kim's knowledge was correct, this maverick union was involved in sweetheart contacts and probably was siphoning off union dues and using brutal tactics to keep the membership in line. It stank.

"Do you have any names, Mr. Smelts?"

"I gave it to you when you first came in here. Rustman. Find Rustman and you got the guy."

CURT FALCONER DROVE his sports car too fast as he thought about what had just happened back in the apartment.

She had called him a goon again. Screw her! He'd locked her in the closet. So what if he was a goon? It put the bread on the table and she never had it so good.

She had pounded on the closet door. What the hell? Let her stay in there for four or five hours and she'd calm down. Then he'd gotten tired of listening to her whimpering and had opened the door and jerked her out so fast she fell across the floor and lay in the corner crying. He'd pulled her clothes from the closet and thrown them in a heap on top of her.

"Get the hell out!"

She'd only sniffled. When he got back tonight, if she was still there, okay. If not, that was okay too. So, maybe he was a goon—whatever the hell that was. It beat delivering beer kegs to sleazy bars all day. The college football scholarship had looked good at the time, with maybe a shot at the pros four years later, but he couldn't cut the classroom crap no matter how painlessly they tried to set it up. He'd played the one season and had never gone back. That was followed by two seasons with a semipro team in Waterville, and then the beer deliveries for a distributor—rolling kegs into bars eight hours a day—and no real dough at that.

The deal with Smelts had worked out beautifully. He and Mike had worked the local unions where Smelts sent them. After a few days on the job, trouble had always ceased.

That was until the last time. Somebody had gotten to Maginacolda in the middle of the night and wasted him. Falconer shifted in the seat of the convertible and felt the weight of the .38 holstered under his left arm. They wouldn't get him that way. He'd take over where Mike left off and get the local back in the union where it belonged. With Rustman gone that wouldn't be difficult.

He turned off Route 98 and went down the secondary road that led toward the Murphysville Convalescent Home. As the car rounded a bend, Falconer saw a truck stopped in the road. A man in a red safety vest waved a flag at him until he braked the car.

The man with the flag climbed back into the cab of the dump truck and began slowly to back up the large vehicle. With each gear shift the rear of the inclined bed truck seemed to inch closer to his car.

If that bastard backed too far and brushed the hood of the Corvette, he'd break his face.

The truck continued backing and he leaned on the horn until it stopped. He slammed from the car as the driver left the truck cab. Falconer stood on the pavement near the rear of the truck and tried to place the familiar-looking truck driver. The large sunglasses obscured most of the driver's face, but still . . .

"Move your fucking truck!"

The man in the sunglasses smiled before he jumped back in the cab. "Sure."

The voice was familiar. Something moved over his head. He looked up.

The rear of the dump truck, angled directly over his head, opened. He tried to throw himself to the side, but fifteen tons of dirt and rock caught him across the back and buried him.

5

Lyon Wentworth rode in terror. His body was rigid as his hands pushed against the cruiser's dashboard. His legs were braced stiffly in the well. "You're exceeding the speed limit," he said hoarsely.

Rocco drove with tantalizing nonchalance. One bullish elbow protruded out the window while his other hand lightly held the steering wheel. "The state boys respect a badge."

As if in acknowledgment, a state police car passed in the far lane. Its horn signal of recognition faded quickly as the two cars accelerated past each other. Lyon tried to ignore the speedometer that hovered near eighty and to concentrate on the recent meeting with Jason Smelts. The union leader's conviction that Marty Rustman was responsible for Maginacolda's murder didn't fit his own theory that Fabian Bunting's death was due to her having seen Rustman's kidnapping. If Rustman were dead, who killed Maginacolda? Kim was now acting head of the union, and it was impossible to believe that their friend was responsible for some strange internecine war between the opposing unions.

"Pat is convinced that the robbery of the cash at Kim's union was an inside job," Rocco said.

"How's that?"

"Whoever broke in there knew exactly where the money was kept."

Lyon tried to fit that in with the other known facts of the case. In a sense, everything that had happened seemed to be a series of unrelated events, but he had the feeling that somewhere there was an interrelating factor, and that all that happened was, in fact, interconnected. A conflict between two unions, a good guy disappears and a bad one is murdered . . .

Rocco turned off Route 98 onto the secondary road that led toward Murphysville. Lyon saw a parked dump truck ahead. Its rear compartment was tilted upward and tons of dirt had spewed over the road. Parked behind the truck was an empty Corvette. Several sawhorses had been pulled off to the side of the road.

Rocco slowed down to swerve around the sports car and truck and then jockeyed back into the right lane. Fifty yards down the road past the two parked vehicles he jammed on the brakes. The police car fishtailed for a dozen yards as Rocco spun the wheel into a bootlegger's turn and drove back to the truck.

"What's up?" Lyon yelled over the screech of protesting tires.

"That's the stolen dump truck I've been looking for." Rocco slammed on the brakes again and slid from the driver's seat in a quick fluid motion. He crouched with pulled service revolver as he walked carefully toward the two vehicles.

Lyon waited until his friend had warily circled the truck and convertible before he left the car. Rocco holstered his gun and climbed into the cab.

Lyon walked around the truck and stood before the massive pile of dirt that had spilled across a complete lane of the road. He looked up into the empty bin of the truck, and then at the Corvette parked a few feet away. The sports car driver's door was open and the keys were still in the ignition.

He could understand teen-agers stealing a truck on a lark, and perhaps even inadvertently or purposefully dumping its load onto the pavement, but what about the sports car with its keys still in the ignition? The barriers that were now pushed off to the side might account for the sports car stopping. Its driver might have stepped out to investigate. Perhaps he stood by the rear of the dump truck and then . . .

Lyon rushed around the truck and wrenched a shovel from

52

brackets by the side of the cab. He began to shovel at the large mound of dirt. Soil and rocks flew to either side as he frantically tried to clear the large pile.

Rocco climbed down from the cab and stood watching. "Just what in hell are you doing?"

"A shovel, Rocco. . . . See if there's another one on the truck. Help me! I think there's someone under here."

THE ASSISTANT MEDICAL EXAMINER kneeling by the body looked up at Rocco with a frown that changed into deep bewilderment. "Well?" Rocco asked.

"Nothing's final until a complete examination, but I would say death by suffocation." The doctor looked back down at the dirt-covered body and then stood. "Odd, isn't it, Chief? Two in a row like this."

Police cars, an ambulance, and a tow truck cluttered the narrow road. Uniformed officers began to make order out of chaos. Shortly the parked vehicles would be removed, a highway crew would begin removal of the dirt, and the tree-shaded road would return to normal. A second man dead of suffocation. Lyon knew there was a connection with the other murders.

THE PHONE WAS RINGING when Bea entered the side door. She put the cardboard box filled with seedling tomato plants down on the kitchen counter and reached for the phone.

"Beatrice?"

"Is that you, Collie?"

"As ever, darling. I thought you might like to know that the governor called and wanted to know what my intentions are for the convention."

"I knew she'd be interested in who you were backing for the U.S. Senate."

"No, dear. She was interested in the state senate. Your old seat which I now occupy."

Bea felt her palms turn clammy. It shouldn't be important. She had no right to expect any such gift. "And?" She tried to appear

53

nonchalant. When she had vacated her senate seat to run for secretary of the state, she had hoped that Collie would step aside if she ever wanted to run again.

"I suppose you're interested in running, Bea?"

Bea had tried to tell herself that she wasn't interested. She had tried to convince herself that the house and Lyon needed her exclusive presence, but she didn't believe it. She wanted her old seat back. She wanted it back very much. "Well, Collie. You've had it for two terms and at one point you said you weren't interested in staying in the state house."

"I've been under severe pressure, Bea. And I do hope you understand. Certain people are insistent that I run again. If you insist on trying, I will have to fight you."

Bea concluded the conversation as quickly and politely as she could and then slumped on a kitchen stool. It hurt. My God, it hurt. She had hoped that Collie would step aside gracefully and assure her of the nomination without a floor fight. Now there would be a battle. She would have to fight tooth and claw for what she wanted.

The day turned darker.

It was nearly an hour later when she realized that the sound of typing coming from Lyon's study was clattering at the fastest clip she had ever heard. At least that was one positive item in her life.

She slipped from the stool and left the kitchen for the study. An unfamiliar feminine figure was hunched over the typewriter. The woman at the machine seemed to be in her late thirties. There was an aura of the displaced about her, as if her features were slightly off-center. Her long hair hung down behind her in an incongruous braid.

Bea automatically adjusted her hearing aid and cleared her throat. The typing ceased immediately and the woman whirled on the swivel chair and pushed back against the desk as if frightened.

A hundred political rallies and ten thousand handshakes forced Bea's smile as she extended her hand and stepped forward. "I'm Bea Wentworth."

"Mandy Summers. Mr. Wentworth hired me to retype his book."
The woman clasped her hands tightly as if afraid of physical contact.

"He seems to have chosen well. From what I heard, you are very fast."

"They taught me to type as part of my rehabilitation. I'm supposed to tell any employer immediately that I'm on parole."

"Oh?" Bea was startled by the remark.

"I'm a murderess."

Bea caught herself before the automatic "that's nice" was articulated. For an inexplicable and inappropriate reason she wanted to reply that she was a Capricorn. She took a closer look at the self-professed murderess. The features were somewhat familiar, but she couldn't place them. She met many people during her political campaigns, but had never developed the Jim Farley ability of never forgetting a face or name.

"I hope you don't mind," Mandy Summers continued in a small voice.

"No, of course not," Bea replied and somehow felt that reply was also inadequate. She heard the front door open as Lyon and Kim entered.

Bea found them in the former game room that now housed her files and a Ping-Pong table covered with books and news clippings. One wall was covered with a large map. Lyon stood before the map in deep thought.

"There's a murderess in our study, Lyon."

"Yes, of course." He drew a circle on the map.

Bea turned to Kim. "Do you know anything about this?"

"I'm just here to stick pins in maps," Kim said. "He says we'll talk when Rocco gets here."

"I mean about our typist. LYON!"

"Hi, dear." He turned away from the map. "I hired a typist to redo the manuscript. It will give me time to devote to the case." He used a compass to draw a larger circle on the map.

"She says she's a murderess."

"That's right. She is."

"Killed her husband," Kim said.

"With a knife," Lyon added.

"A knife?" Bea said.

"Butcher knife, wasn't it, Kim?"

"I think so. They found him in the kitchen."

"We're helping to rehabilitate her."

The sound of Rocco's cruiser in the driveway was unmistakable. In seconds the large police officer was in the room waving a Teletype flimsy. "We've got an ID on him."

"Rocco, do you know anything about Mrs. Summers who is now in our study?"

"Hi, Bea. She was released from the Niantic Women's Prison last week."

"Should I lock up the knives?"

"Come on, Bea. You know better than that. The recidivism rate for that type of crime is almost nil."

Lyon took the flimsy from Rocco. "Six prior arrests."

"Right. All for assault. Almost all of them involved union activities."

"Mrs. Summers had six arrests before . . ."

"I think we're on different wavelengths," Kim said.

"WILL SOMEONE TELL ME WHAT WE'RE TALKING ABOUT AND WHY?"

"Falconer," Rocco said.

"And who is Falconer?"

"The one who was killed by the dump truck," Kim said.

"That explains everything. I've got a murderess in my study and a man called Falconer was run over by a dump truck."

"Smothered, actually," Lyon said.

"It fell on him?"

"About fifteen tons of good topsoil did."

"The way it breaks out," Rocco said, "Curt Falconer was on his way to the Murphysville Convalescent Home to take Maginacolda's place Someone got to him on the road where we found him."

"And he had a record for assault," Lyon said pensively. "That's interesting." He sat back in a canvas captain's chair, stretched out his legs, and began to stare at the ceiling.

Kim took Bea by the arm and led her to the cracked leather couch in the corner. "Rocco and Lyon found him. The body, I mean. They were driving back from Hartford . . ."

As Kim brought Bea up to date, Rocco examined the map tacked on the wall. It was a large U.S. geodetic survey map of the Murphysville area. He tried to make sense out of the lines Lyon had drawn.

"Have you talked to anyone at the nursing home? Did they expect Falconer?"

"They did. And we phoned the union. Smelts is the one who ordered Falconer out here."

"Suffocating a man under a load of dirt is a strange way to kill someone."

"No more so than burying him in concrete."

"I think I have a scenario," Lyon said.

"Try us."

"We have every reason to believe that the union run by Jason Smelts is a sweetheart deal. They make beneficial contracts with management."

"I'll vouch for that," Kim said vehemently.

"The union was attacked by Marty Rustman. Smelts fought back but lost. Then Marty disappears."

"Which at this point has just about broken the strike," Kim added.

"We know that nearly simultaneously with his disappearance, Dr. Bunting was placed in the tub and killed."

"Because she saw something."

"What did she see? We know she was in the sun-room with a pair of opera glasses. Immediately below the sun-room is a walled courtyard where a van was parked. Let us assume that Rustman was forcibly put into the van and driven off."

"Which was seen by Bunting."

"Yes, but she in turn was also seen by one of the abductors."

"Abductors?" Kim snorted. "No one's been abducted since the nineteenth century."

"Snatched," Rocco said.

"One of the snatchers sees Bunting watching them, and he goes inside to kill her because she might have recognized him."

"It would also have to be someone who was familiar with the interior of the home," Bea said.

"Probably Maginacolda. He would have access to the home without difficulty."

"It's hard to imagine that the old lady has a team of cohorts who are running around sticking people in concrete for revenge."

"No, not Bunting's friends." Lyon turned toward the map. "If Rustman was in the van that the strikers saw leave the home, it would have turned to the right, away from the main part of town. The area to the west is mostly state park."

"A good place to dump a body."

"Now, follow me. The van drives to this area." Lyon's hand made a sweep over the map.

"There are thousands of acres of woods there."

"That's going to make it difficult to find, but let me continue. As nearly as we can determine, the strikers saw the van leave the nursing home about the time Dr. Bunting was killed."

"Which means at least two people were involved."

"They had to lure Marty Rustman into the courtyard and knock him out. There must have been at least two men involved."

"I think three," Lyon said. "Look at it this way. Rustman was probably knocked out, tied, and gagged. He might have awakened and been able to thrash around in the back of the van. That would increase their risk of detection—unless, the driver of the van stopped somewhere to pick up another accomplice."

"Logical enough."

"A third man got into the van and they took Rustman to a secluded spot in the state forest where they tried to kill him."

"Tried?"

58

"It's possible they didn't succeed. That somehow Rustman survived."

"Buried alive," Bea said.

"Shot and put in a shallow grave."

Rocco looked dubious. "Shot but not killed. He manages to extricate himself from the grave and returns to get rid of the men who tried to kill him."

"I think we can safely assume that Maginacolda was involved, and since he needed help, Curt Falconer would be a logical choice."

"This could be tied to the theft of the union money," Kim said. "Marty knew where it was, of course. If he needed working capital, but didn't want anyone to know he was alive . . ."

Rocco's fist slammed against the map. "This is all wild conjecture. I can't run an investigation based on a man returning from the grave to knock people off."

"Doesn't the method of death in the last two killings tell you something?"

"That dump truck could have been an accident. A couple of kids could have stolen the truck, dumped it accidentally, and then run away."

"Do you really believe that?"

"No."

"For a man who had been buried alive, it would be a fitting way to get revenge."

"If your theory of the third man is correct, someone is still alive and walking around waiting for a murder to happen."

"I know," Lyon said. "There's a third man out there somewhere and Rustman could be trying to kill him—to suffocate him."

"What do we do now?"

"I'd like Kim to keep an eye on the union office. It's a natural place for Rustman to return to for sleep. Is any food there?"

"Cold cuts, soda, beer, things like that."

"Will you keep an eye on the office, Kim?"

"Right."

"I think Bea ought to go back and see Rustman's wife. He's liable to make contact with her or the children."

"Do you have any assignments for the local police authorities, sir?"

"Sarcastic, Rocco?"

"Dubious. But okay, what do we do?"

"Search for the grave."

SOME MEN ARE tweedy no matter what the fabric of their clothing. It is a quality of pose and attitude, a nuance of thoughtfulness before a reply, a hesitation of speech often punctuated with a pipe. Ronald Thornton of the State Department of Environmental Protection was such a man.

Lyon felt at ease with this type. He had participated in many departmental conferences during his teaching career, and those meetings were always well attended by such individuals. Bea's call to the commissioner had arranged the appointment, and Lyon had wandered the dim halls of the old State Office Building for half an hour before being directed to the correct office.

"I understand you're interested in SCORP, Mr. Wentworth."

"Is that a bird?"

There was a thoughtful pause as Lyon's remark was processed within some inner workings of Thornton's mind. The eventual chuckle was muted and quickly silenced. "SCORP, that's the State of Connecticut Outdoor Recreation Plan—my baby."

"Actually, I want to find out the traffic count and usage of certain areas in the Nahung State Forest."

"Nahung. Interesting piece of property. Undeveloped, of course."

"You must have some information concerning it."

"Of course. That's where SCORP comes in. We do a comprehensive evaluation of every state outdoor recreational facility each year."

"Nahung's been undeveloped for the last twenty years that I know of. Why reevaluate every year?"

The quick, nontweedy look that Thornton gave Lyon was not of a thoughtful nature, but arose out of the self-protective device that most civil servants maintain as their final defense mechanism. "I suppose you need this informaion for some project Senator Wentworth is involved in?"

"In a manner of speaking. Is there anything you can tell me about the Nahung forest?"

"Let's see what we have." There was a careful shuffling of files until Thornton found the appropriate one. "Nahung, yes. We acquired it from the Valley Water Company in 1940. We allow hunting during the season and also give a number of wood-cutting permits during the winter months. Several small streams, no other bodies of water of any size, except of course, the forest does run down to the Connecticut River."

"Do you have any traffic counts or camper usage figures?"

"Since we don't have forestry personnel out there, we can't allow camping. Too much of a fire hazard. That's not to say that there isn't unauthorized camping in the area."

"You do run counts. I mean, hikers use the land, dirt bikers, bird watchers, and that sort of thing?"

"We like to feel that these lands are held for the people in a sacred trust."

"Then you do run traffic counts?"

"The youngest is three years old."

"That would help."

"It would be easier, Mr. Wentworth, if I knew exactly what you were trying to find out?"

"There are dozens of old roads and logging trails crossing the forest. I need to know which ones are passable by a van-type vehicle. The roads I am most interested in would have a low traffic count."

"We don't have the figures for every logging road and trail in a state forest."

"I know you don't, but logging roads and fire roads eventually connect with paved secondary roads. It is those junctions that will give me the information I need."

Thornton shuffled over his desk for another file. "I think we can give you some information." He began to write figures on a map as Lyon peered over his shoulder.

IN HARTFORD, Bea turned off Park onto Nieman Boulevard and drove toward the Rustman home. She unconsciously slowed down as she attempted to put her thoughts in order and decide on the best approach to use on Barbara Rustman. When she was a block from the house, she saw a teen-age girl with a long blond ponytail going up the Rustman walk. The front door opened as Barbara Rustman came out on the stoop to greet the girl.

Bea slowed the Datsun to a stop at the curb three houses up from the Rustmans'. Barbara seemed in a hurry, as indicated by a slightly forward bend to her body and the hasty conversation with the young girl. Although Bea could not hear the words, the older woman was obviously giving instructions to the younger.

The girl entered the house and waved to Barbara, who hurried to a five-year-old Chevrolet parked in the driveway. She backed out without looking and turned down the street in the opposite direction from Bea.

The young girl was obviously a baby-sitter. Barbara Rustman was going somewhere that was quite important to her. Bea started the Datsun and pulled away from the curb.

She had once heard Rocco explain to Lyon the rules for car surveillance. At the time she hadn't been interested enough to pay much attention. Until this moment she couldn't recall following anyone. At least not since grade school when some boys down the street refused to let her come to their hidden clubhouse. In that instance she'd been easily detected. Didn't Rocco say that you should let another car intervene between you and the subject? Yes. She dropped back and let a red Camaro get between her car and Rustman's.

The Chevrolet turned into a shopping center and pulled into a parking space in front of a supermarket.

Bea slammed the steering wheel in frustration. She had been sure that Barbara was going somewhere important, that she had an appointment, or perhaps even a meeting with her husband. She watched the other woman hurry from the car and go into the store.

Bea took a kerchief from her pocketbook and tied it over her head. Wide sunglasses from the glove compartment completed her disguise. She hoped the simple subterfuge would be sufficient, but she suspected that her appearance in the store was so out of context for Mrs. Rustman that she would barely be noticed. She waited until two women with small children entered the store before she followed.

Barbara was performing the fastest shopping expedition that Bea had ever witnessed. The woman seemed frantic as she wheeled her cart in and out between other shoppers and snatched a haphazard assortment of goods from the shelves. When Barbara wheeled into the check-out line, Bea abandoned her cart and slipped out of the store.

She sat in the Datsun mentally cataloging the items the other woman had purchased. There were canned goods, fruit, and fast foods—food for a husband in hiding or quick meals for a harried mother of two children.

Barbara Rustman put her groceries into the backseat of the Chevy and drove quickly from the parking lot with Bea not far behind.

Two miles further on, the Chevrolet pulled into the parking lot of a motel. Bea drove past, made a U-turn in a gas station, and went past the motel a second time. Barbara had left her car and was knocking on the door of the second unit from the far end. Bea drove past as the motel door was opened.

She made another turn at a McDonald's franchise and drove back to the motel. She parked in the far corner of the lot and slouched in her seat to watch the room Barbara had entered. She was convinced that Marty Rustman was in there with his wife.

It was an hour and a half later when the couple emerged from the room. Barbara hurried to her car as the man walked toward a large Buick.

Gustav Tanner, the nursing home administrator, walked with a small man's strut as he climbed into his car.

6

IT WAS uncomfortable standing in the back of a pickup truck as it thumped over rutted dirt roads. Patrolman Jamie Martin drove while Rocco and Lyon stood in the truck bed, held on to the cab roof, and looked to each side. They had been searching for the grave for five hours, and Lyon's ankles had begun to hurt from the constant jouncing over rough roads. The minor roads crisscrossing the state forest seemed endless.

Rocco was tight-lipped, grim, and reminded Lyon of an alert Roman centurion leading his phalanx through some deep forest in Gaul.

Rocco thumped on the roof of the truck cab and Jamie Martin brought the vehicle to a quick halt, which almost threw Lyon over the roof onto the hood. The uniformed officer slammed from the truck and looked up at his chief.

"See something?"

"Hell, no! My legs hurt."

Lyon looked over at his friend gratefully. They both stepped down from the back of the truck and walked briskly back and forth to unwind their knotted muscles.

"Well?" Rocco said.

"We could have missed it. The forest is thick in parts, and if it was more than a few yards from the side of the road, we'd miss it."

"Or if they covered the grave with leaves, we'd never see it either."

Lyon reached inside the cab for the map that lay on the seat. He examined it closely until he located their position. "How many miles have we covered so far?"

"About thirty, Mr. Wentworth."

Lyon looked up at the sky. The sun had dipped beneath the tree tops. In minutes deep shadows would fall across the forest floor and obscure their vision. "We'll continue for another fifteen minutes and then we'll have to come back tomorrow to finish."

"You've got an interesting theory, Lyon. I know you've done your homework in picking out the roadways to search, but I have other business back in town. I can't spend another day out here."

"I'll get Kim and Bea to help. I appreciate the time you've put in so far, Rocco."

"Appreciate, hell! It's my job." He leaped back onto the truck bed with an agility that surprised Lyon.

The truck began its ponderous, lumbering way down the narrow logging road. Lyon was afraid that they were faced with a nearly impossible job. He recalled an incident in this forest four years ago when a light plane had crashed. The pilot had been killed and the body had remained undetected for five months before a group of scouts accidentally stumbled upon the wreckage. If Rustman's abductors had been careful and gone at least a hundred yards into the woods, they would never locate the grave. He could only hope that they were impatient men who were undisciplined and afraid of being detected. In that instance they may have dug a shallow grave only a few feet from the side of the road. They may have assumed that the natural fall of leaves would obliterate any evidence of the grave.

Rocco thumped on the roof of the cab. The truck swerved to a halt as the right front wheel sank into a deep hole. Jamie Martin stuck his head out the window. "See something, Chief?"

"Back up to that birch."

"Birch?"

"That white tree back there."

The patrolman threw the truck in reverse. The wheels spun uselessly for a moment, and they could smell burning rubber before the truck lurched out of the hole and backed up. Before the truck came to a full stop, Rocco vaulted over the side and ran toward the woods.

Lyon followed and caught up to Rocco who stared down at the edge of a rock by the birch tree. A piece of rope lay at the base of the rock. Along a sharp edge of the stone were dark stains. He lifted the severed rope with the edge of his pencil and dropped it into a small acetate bag. "The way I see it, someone rubbed that rope against the rock until it broke."

"His arms would have been tied behind his back."

"He'd have to sit with his back against the sharp edge and rub. It would have taken a long time."

"Over here, Chief."

Jamie Martin stood by a small pit partially filled with dirt. It was three feet deep and the length of a man.

"I think we've found it," Lyon said.

Martin looked puzzled as he stared into the pit. "But there's no one in it."

"There was."

SARGE'S PLACE WAS a dim bar utterly devoid of redeeming features, but they felt comfortable in its dingy ambience. The owner, retired sergeant Renfroe, had served under Rocco in the army, and the relationship between the two still existed. Lyon had once attempted to define his own predilection for the place. He had noted the absence of any omniscient television screen, counted the fact that Sarge always kept a bottle of Dry Sack under the bar for him, and then stopped. He and Rocco were just used to the place.

They'd driven from the state forest to police headquarters, where Rocco had put out an APB for Marty Rustman, and then continued on to the bar in separate vehicles. They slipped into their usual booth and Sarge brought the sherry in a pony for Lyon and a large tumbler of vodka and ice water for Rocco.

Rocco looked up at his old sergeant with concern. "If you looked any better, Renfroe, you'd have a lily planted on your chest."

"It's drinking all that customers buy me, Captain. Does terrible things to a man."

"A man's liver, too."

"If I stopped drinking now, my liver would become unpickled and probably kill me." Sarge shuffled off, drew a short beer from the tap, downed it in one gulp, and belched.

Rocco and Lyon stared into their drinks and then simultaneously raised their glasses. Rocco leaned back in the booth and stretched his legs. "The bastard's run amok."

"It would seem so. What are the odds on picking him up?"

Rocco shrugged. "It depends on how careful he is. Pasquale will have the Rustman house staked out. He'll also cover union head-quarters and will watch Rustman's friends and acquaintances. Sometimes a guy who tries to drop out of sight will take off for another part of the country."

"He obviously hasn't."

"Then he'll contact someone. He'll surface eventually. I think the guy's around the bend."

"It must have been a horrifying experience when you consider he was kidnapped, probably knifed or shot, and then buried."

They watched their drinks as if the future movements of Marty Rustman would be revealed in them. "The question is, how many more is he going to get before he's caught?"

Lyon finished his sherry and looked toward the bar to catch Sarge Renfroe's attention. "At least one more."

"How's that?"

"I believe that two men grabbed Marty at the nursing home, but one of them went back inside to kill Dr. Bunting."

"Maginacolda."

"Exactly. I think the man who drove the van needed help. He stopped somewhere for a third man."

"Who will be the next victim?"

"Yes, whoever he is." Sarge swayed toward them with another

round of drinks. "By the way, what will happen to Kim on the assault charge?"

"I've arranged with the prosecutor for a thirty-day suspended."

"I guess that's the best that can be expected."

They were quiet. Each man understood the need not to talk as they temporarily dwelt in private places with private thoughts. As Lyon looked at his friend hunched over his vodka, he saw the Wobblies perched on each of Rocco's shoulders. The outline of his monsters was faint. Their forms were barely distinguishable, but they looked at their creator with sad eyes.

Lyon did not think that he would be able to write another book. A part of him knew that this was fallacious, that he had felt like this before; but it was still depressing. The last book was finished and was now in the quick hands of Mandy Summers. He should be thinking about the next, outlining possible ideas, writing portions of important scenes, and talking to his editor about a new contract. But literary matters seemed unimportant in light of his increasing involvement in the recent bizarre events. The situation had sapped his creative energy and consumed his emotions. He knew that he would have to stay with the investigation until it was complete. Only its final solution would release him from the obsession. Then the Wobblies might return.

Rocco Herbert was fatigued. He wanted to quit the force. He was tired of scraping motorcyclists off the pavement with a spoon, tired of the daily trips to the local discount store to pick up teen-age shoplifters, tired of night stakeouts to ambush old men who revealed their shriveled instruments to young women on dark streets. In times past he had considered running for town clerk, but the incumbent seemed intent on dying in office. Perhaps one day, when the present town clerk passed on to the great record vault in the sky. He hoped it wouldn't be too long.

"How much have they had to drink?" It was a faraway feminine voice.

"Not much, Senator Wentworth. You know that Lyon only has a pony or two of sherry. And the captain only drinks ice water."

"Renfroe?"

"Well, maybe a little vodka laced in once in a while. But they've only had one."

"Sarge?"

"Maybe four or five, Senator. That's all. Honest."

The two men turned to look up at Bea standing by the booth. "Hi, hon."

"Let me have a dry martini, Sarge."

"Yes, ma'am."

Bea slipped into the booth next to Lyon. She thought she heard Sarge Renfroe mumbling under his breath about women in bars, but she was too tired to take up the feminist cudgels, and Sarge was past redemption in that area anyway. "Are you two conscious?"

"We are not sloshed. Merely contemplative."

"I'll take your word for it. By the way, Marty Rustman's wife has a thing going with Gustav Tanner."

"Tanner?"

"I followed her to a motel where she met him."

"Could it have been for other reasons?"

"They pulled the blinds and were in there an hour and a half."

It happened ten minutes later. Lyon had finished telling Bea about their discovery of the grave when Rocco's attention was drawn to the bar. He never knew whether it was some subtle intonation in Sarge's voice or a blurred movement he caught from the corner of his eye. He was instantly alert as he shifted imperceptibly toward the edge of the booth.

Rocco looked over the edge of the booth toward the bar. Sarge's eyes were wide with fear as he stood stiffly before a man on the other side of the bar. Renfroe nodded and then turned to open the cash register. He began to scoop bills from each of the drawer's compartments.

"Hurry," Rocco heard the customer say.

He slipped from the seat and hunched forward. His right hand drew the .44 Magnum holstered at the left side of his waist.

Bea looked frightened and Lyon put his hand over hers.

Rocco took three strides across the room with his pistol held in both hands. "Easy, son, easy, and we'll all be okay."

Lyon turned to shield Bea. The robber's gun became visible as he brought it up from his side and pointed it directly at Renfroe's head.

"He goes first," the man said.

"Drop it," Rocco replied softly.

The man spun on his heels as the gun wavered toward Rocco. The barrel of Rocco's gun caught him across the cheekbone and split the flesh in a long gash as the momentum of the blow knocked him sideways and across the floor.

Rocco's left foot slammed on the fallen man's gun hand while his right kicked into the stomach. He knelt and tore handcuffs from his belt and cuffed the man's hands behind him. He grabbed the bandit's shirt collar and dragged him across the floor and out the door.

There was stunned silence in the bar. Sarge Renfroe poured himself a stiff drink with trembling hands. "The captain's one tough bastard, isn't he, Mr. Wentworth?"

"Yes, he is," Lyon replied and remembered the pain-saddened look on Rocco's face as he shoved the man out the door.

THE FRONT DOOR of Jason Smelts's union headquarters was locked, and Lyon nearly turned away in disappointment until he heard voices inside. He banged on the door and someone unlocked it. When he stepped inside, the man turned and called toward the rear of the building, "Here's another one."

"Smelts is recruiting a goddamn army."

Lyon followed the man who had opened the door into Smelts's office where five men sat with open cans of beer. It was difficult to tell if they were celebrating, commiserating, or merely avoiding a return home. They eyed Lyon speculatively. There was a similarity among the men in the room. Each of them seemed to have a thick neck with broad shoulders and large arms. Although they were boisterous, there was a stony cast to their faces and their eyes were cool.

"What they call you?"

"Wentworth, Lyon."

"Which local you taking over?"

"How would he know? He ain't been elected yet."

Laughter.

"I want to see Jason Smelts."

A large man sitting astride Smelts's desk signaled to a man across the room and a beer can flipped toward him. He opened it and drank in long draughts and continued a story he had begun before Lyon arrived. "So, anyway, the kid gets up at the organizational meeting and says some shit like, 'I move the previous question.' Smelts was fit to be tied and gave me the sign. I walked over to the kid and cold-cocked him. He slid down under his seat and kept on going till he was flat on the floor."

Laughter. More beer cans were flipped around the room.

"You know, Wendworse, you don't seem mean enough for this kinda work?"

"Wentworth."

"You ever go to some bastard's house and offer to break his knees with a baseball bat if he didn't cooperate?"

Lyon realized that not only had he not used such persuasion, but the prospect had never occurred to him. As he looked from one face to another in the room, he decided that an ingenuous manner was not in his present best interests. "I have my methods," he replied quietly.

A head in the far corner nodded. "I had a guy like him with me out in Youngstown once. Those quiet types can fool you."

Other heads nodded and looked toward Lyon with a respect that one professional holds for another.

"Where's Smelts?" Lyon asked.

"Has a date over at the Clock and Chime on Third Street. Said he'd be back after he jumped her."

"I want to see him."

"I wouldn't bother Jason when he's with a broad."

Lyon walked toward the door. "He'll talk to me."

"See what I mean about those quiet kind," a voice from behind him said as he left the union headquarters.

The Clock and Chime was a lounge only a few blocks away and

71

was one of those remote bars found in every city that are inhabited by a classless sort of clientele. The customers are well dressed, always in possession of money, and wander in and out at odd hours that do not correspond to the usual off-hours of the gainfully employed.

Lyon entered the dim interior and took a seat on a stool halfway down the bar. Three men on his left were playing liar's poker with dollar bills. It was a game whose rules he only vaguely understood. A bartender in a red-striped apron with white shirt sleeves puffed to the elbows and held by elastic garters served Lyon a house sherry. He tasted it and tried not to grimace.

The bar mirror was an ancient affair of clouded glass with train stickers of long-forgotten railways pasted along its edge. Lyon saw the reflected image of Jason Smelts in a booth in the far corner of the lounge. The union leader was huddled close to a very young woman. The girl had a pouty prettiness, but she seemed too young for the lounge. Then he remembered that the drinking age in Connecticut had been lowered to eighteen, the probable age of the girl.

Jason Smelts leered and seemed to envelop the girl. His arm was around her shoulder and he looked at her with a lust that was so apparent it filled that corner of the lounge.

Lyon ordered another sherry and slid off the stool. As he approached the booth, Jason Smelts squinted in annoyance. Lyon pulled a chair from another table and sat down.

"Wentworth," Smelts said with obvious distaste.

"I thought we should talk about Marty."

"See me tomorrow in the office."

"Who is this creep?" were the first jarring words from the girl.

"A cop from Murphysville."

"Oh." Her pout increased. "I'm eighteen."

"Rustman's alive," Lyon said.

Dissembling is a learned response. With age and experience the facial mask can harden and become nearly impregnable. It was obvious that Smelts had built up such a façade over the years, but Lyon's remark shocked and penetrated his attempt to appear nonchalant. He rocked back in his seat as if he'd been hit. The response lasted only a moment before his hand snaked out to lift the glass. He took a casual sip. "So? I told you Marty was the bad guy."

"There's more to it than that."

"How?"

"I'd like you to consider a hypothetical situation."

"A what?"

"A possible version of what might have happened."

"You trying to lay something on me?"

"Do you want to hear?"

"I got nothing better to do." He looked over at the young woman. "Make it snappy."

"Let us suppose that Marty Rustman was taken from the convalescent home by Maginacolda and Curt Falconer. The two men who were subsequently killed."

"What are you driving at?"

"Let us say that the van that took Marty away stopped and picked up a third man."

"I don't like games, Wentworth." He looked down at a large jeweled watch just below his French cuffs. "You got ten seconds to finish and then amscray."

"Two of the men involved in the kidnapping are dead."

Smelts raised a finger and a waiter immediately refilled his glass. "I never been to college, but I see where you're going. Rustman, or somebody else, is going to take care of that third guy. If that was the way it happened, which it isn't."

The girl plucked at Smelts's sleeve. "We got to get goin', Jasie. I get home after midnight and my dad beats the living daylight out of me."

Smelts ignored her.

"I think you have it, Mr. Smelts. The third man is in danger. Do you know who he is?"

"You got to be kidding? If I knew something like that, I'd be involved in conspiracy to whatever happened to Rustman."

"The man's life depends on it."

"Anybody that could snatch Rustman, if he was snatched, can take care of himself."

"Falconer carried a gun and fifteen tons of dirt killed him."

"Careless."

"I don't know how to impress upon you the importance of finding that third man."

The girl plucked at Smelts's sleeve again. "Come on, Jason. I'll show you a good time."

Jason looked annoyed and pulled a money clip from his pocket and flipped a bill at her. "Beat it."

The girl glared. "You want me to go?"

"Jesus! They don't even understand English nowadays. Beat it, and on the way out tell Morrie I want a phone—fast."

The girl slouched from the booth and talked briefly to the bartender as she left the lounge. A phone was delivered and jacked into the floor near the booth. Smelts began to dial. "The cops think Marty's alive?"

"That he could be."

Smelts held the phone over his ear and Lyon could hear the ring. He held a hand over the receiver. "Out, Wentworth! Now!"

Lyon left the booth and returned to the bar. He could see the mirror image of Smelts on the phone. "Morrie."

"Yes, sir."

"Smelts wants me on an extension."

"There's one plugged in over there."

"Thanks." Lyon went to the booth with the phone and turned sideways on the seat to hide his actions from the bartender's view and quickly unscrewed the receiver plate before lifting the phone.

"I wouldn't have called if it weren't important, Mrs. Truman."

Lyon was surprised at the obsequious tone in Smelts's voice.

"The phone could be tapped. You know your instructions."

"Yes, ma'am. But something has come up."

"For your sake, Jason, it had better be important."

"The cops think Rustman is alive."

"That's impossible."

"It can happen. People get careless."

"You know I don't want to hear details like that."

"I'm sorry. I wouldn't bother you except that maybe he's coming after me."

"Nonsense." The feminine voice was devoid of feeling. She spoke with a flat and emotionless tone tinged with annoyance.

"He's already gotten Mike and Curt."

"You're an idiot, Smelts."

"I want to get out of town for a while. Maybe go to Florida for a couple of months."

"You leave here and you'll regret it. I promise you that."

"You don't know what he's done."

"Good-bye, Jason." The connection was broken.

Lyon waited until Smelts hung up before replacing his receiver. He looked over the edge of the booth to see Smelts in the far corner of the lounge. The union leader had his head in his hands.

7

"He kept hurting me, Mrs. Wentworth. I mean, he really beat on me. It got so bad that sometimes I couldn't leave the house because my face was all black and blue." Mandy Summers' eyes glistened as she leaned over the breakfast-nook table.

"Yes, I know, dear. You mentioned it yesterday morning."

"And then he'd threaten to kill me. He had those hunting guns all over the house and he'd point them at me and say he was going to shoot me. It got so that I couldn't stand it. I couldn't sleep. I couldn't do anything."

Bea could only nod, as she'd run out of responses. At the first telling of the story she had felt deep compassion, on the second empathy. At the third recounting she had tried to look for social significance, but subsequent repetitions had drained her of response and dulled her sensitivity. She wondered at Mandy Summers' continued need for daily catharsis.

"And then I couldn't take it anymore. I couldn't stand to have him hurt me again. He'd been drinking and the knife was on the kitchen counter, so I. . ."

It was raining again with an intermittent drizzle that turned green things greener. A heavy mist rose from the river below. There was a change in Mandy's voice that forced Bea's thoughts back to the kitchen.

"Mr. Wentworth said I should ask if there's something I don't understand in the manuscript."

"Try nine-one-one."

"Huh?"

"He's at the police station."

"Oh."

GUSTAV TANNER WAS one of those people who react to a threatening situation with anger. His body communicated hostility by a pronounced forward thrust of the chin and a rigidity of his shoulders.

Rocco reacted to the aggression with pronounced mildness communicated with a Buddha-like expression. Lyon stood at the window looking at the rain while Tanner sat directly in front of the desk.

"I resent your implications! I came here voluntarily in a spirit of cooperation and now you pounce on me with these questions."

"We are concerned about the death of three people," Rocco replied in his quietest manner. "I am sure you and your superiors are also."

"Of course" was the snapped reply.

"I'd like to know your relationship to the deceased."

"She was a patient in the home I manage."

"Rustman?"

"Adversary."

"Explain."

"We had a perfectly satisfactory relationship with another union in the homes until Rustman stirred things up. He agitated the employees until they became dissatisfied and called for an election."

"Which he won."

"Yes. Which was important to me not only in Murphysville, but in the other homes I manage."

"Which meant that once Rustman won here he would go after the other homes?"

"Obviously. It should have been apparent that Rustman was labor and I am management. We were natural enemies, but that doesn't mean that I'd do anything physical to him."

"I didn't say you did."

"That's what you've been implying."

"He's missing."

"So?"

"What about Maginacolda?"

"What about him?"

"He was labor also."

"We had a good working relationship."

"Curt Falconer?"

"I never met the gentleman. I understand he was connected to Mike's union, but I didn't know him personally."

"Barbara Rustman?"

A deep flush spread up Tanner's neck. He sat shock-still for a few moments and then got up from his chair. "Have you been spying on me? Have you been watching my movements? If you have, I think it's a violation of my civil rights."

"Call your attorney."

"I will!" He snatched up the phone from Rocco's desk and held it contemplatively in his hand a moment before slowly replacing the receiver in the cradle. "It isn't convenient for me to call my lawyer at this time."

"Then answer the question," Rocco said offhandedly.

"It's none of your damn business!"

"I think it is."

"Wait a minute! Are you trying to build some sort of case against me because of Rustman's disappearance and Barbara?"

"It's an interesting thought, Mr. Tanner."

"You got it wrong! You've got the whole thing turned upside down. I'm the last person in the world that wants to make waves at this time. I'm involved in a very delicate business maneuver and the last thing I want is any trouble in the home, much less murder."

"Why don't you explain that?"

"It's an extremely confidential matter."

"I am used to keeping confidences, and I am sure you have the word of Mr. Wentworth."

"Of course," Lyon replied.

Tanner sat back in his chair and seemed to calm down. "All right. Not a word beyond this room."

"Unless it is important to the case."

"It isn't, but it is a personal matter that will prove to you that I have nothing to gain from what's been happening."

"Go on."

"I manage a group of convalescent homes for the Shopton Corporation. This company is a miniconglomerate in this state. It owns not only the homes, but a series of other businesses."

"Yes."

"I am a C.P.A., a trained administrator, a good one, if I do say so myself. I am completely qualified to manage the corporation. Now, at the present time, a large block of the stock is held by one individual. The remaining shares are widely dispersed throughout the state. I have worked for a year to obtain proxies on those dispersed shares. I expect, in the very near future, to make a move. In fact, I expect to do so at the next annual meeting, which is in one month's time."

"How does that fit?"

"I certainly do not want people dying of unnatural causes in establishments that I manage. I fully expect to be elected president of the corporation."

"This large block of stock that you are fighting to gain control over, who is it held by?" Lyon asked.

"That's not germane to this discussion."

"It might be. We could check with the secretary of the state's office and determine the probable owner."

"It's held by a woman. A shark."

"A Mrs. Truman."

"How in hell did you know?"

"An educated guess."

Gustav Tanner started for the door. "I assume we have completed our business?"

"Of course," Rocco said blandly.

"Good morning." Tanner left slamming the door.

"Pleasant fellow," Rocco said.

"I think he'd transfer his aged mother to the charity ward."

The phone rang and Rocco picked it up.

Lyon looked out the window as pregnant clouds disgorged further torrents in a sudden burst. Rain fell rapidly and bounced off the parking-lot macadam.

Rocco slammed down the phone. "Damn!"

"What's the matter?"

"The dispatcher just took a call from Henderson's. Possible burglary."

"The funeral home?"

"Goddamn kids took a coffin. I'll see you later."

Rocco stalked from the office. Lyon turned back to look out the window and saw Rocco run through the rain to his cruiser, slam inside, and screech away from the police station.

A funeral home seemed an unlikely place for a burglary. It was unlikely there would be any loose cash around or many items of value that would be hockable. A missing coffin probably meant kids as Rocco suggested. Perhaps something to do with a fraternity hazing.

College was in recess. The summer session hadn't begun yet. Lyon bolted for the door. He ran down the short hall to the rear door and toward his parked pickup.

THE INITIAL ONSLAUGHT of heavy rain had subsided into a heavy drizzle that seemed to have every intention of continuing for hours. Bea Wentworth walked bareheaded in the rain and thought that no matter how beneficial the rain was for her garden, it wasn't helping her depression. She had just finished chastising herself for her insensitivity toward the troubled woman now typing in Lyon's study. Mandy Summers' past problem so overshadowed her own temporary malaise that she felt pangs of guilt for not being able to offer the woman more of herself.

She stood on the patio and viewed the charred Japanese honeysuckle with satisfaction. At least one thing had worked. She watched the slowly moving river below the parapet for a moment, then walked aimlessly toward the stand of pine trees beyond the house.

She turned in curiosity as an unfamiliar car moved up the driveway. A cream-colored Mercedes stopped near the front door. A man's hand reached out and popped an umbrella open before he slid from the car and rang the doorbell.

"Hello," she called and went around the side of the house.

"Hi. Is Senator Wentworth home?"

"Ex-senator Wentworth is standing out in the rain talking to someone." She noticed he was good-looking and wore what Lyon called an ice-cream suit, which was practically color-coordinated with the automobile. Lyon had a suit like that stuffed somewhere deep in the recess of his closet.

He handed her a business card. "I'm Ramsey McLean. I represented Fabian Bunting on a certain matter."

"I see," Bea replied as she looked down at the card with what she expected was a dumb expression. She was astonished at her reaction to the man's physical presence and wished she had worn a kerchief or hat over her head. She knew her hair was a stringy mess and her shoes were muddied. He smiled at her and stepped closer so that the umbrella protected them both.

"It's raining."

"Yes, it is," she said. Her knees were weak. She hadn't had that particular physiological reaction since the summer she was sixteen and had a magnificent crush on the pool lifeguard. The man standing next to her appeared to be her own age. He was as tall as Lyon, although his shoulders were broader. His body tapered to a trim waist. His features were a rugged tan, and a forelock of dark brown hair fell in a casual but carefully coiffured manner.

"I have some business to discuss. It would probably be easier to talk inside."

"Of course. Forgive me." She fumbled with the immobile front doorknob before realizing that it was locked from the inside and her keys hung on the corkboard in the kitchen. "It's locked."

"So I see."

"I came out the kitchen door."

"I would imagine that it's still unlocked then." He smiled and their eyes met.

He accepted her offer of coffee, and she used the time in the kitchen to frantically restore her hair to some semblance of order. When she returned to the living room, she found him at the end of the sofa with an attaché case open on his knees. He took out several legal-sized pages backed with a heavy blue sheet.

"You wanted to discuss something, Mr. McLean?" she asked as she handed him the coffee.

"I'm the attorney for the Murphysville Convalescent Home. A short time ago I was asked to see a patient who requested a lawyer. To explain it simply, Dr. Fabian Bunting requested that I draw up her will."

"She never had one before?"

"Evidently not. She doesn't seem to have any near relatives."

"How does this concern me?"

"You are the beneficiary."

"I'm astounded. Dr. Bunting was a teacher of mine years ago. We corresponded occasionally, but I hadn't really spent any time with her until recently when she was hospitalized here."

"Nevertheless, it was her express wish that you inherit what she had."

"I'm sure it can't be much. I think it would be appropriate that I sign it over to the college I attended and where she taught."

"That's your decision, of course. According to my inventory and a rough guess at final expenses, taxes, and fees, there should be a net worth remaining of approximately ninety-two thousand dollars."

"How much?"

"A bit less than one hundred thousand dollars."

"It's hard to believe that she had that much. I had always thought that her only income was a pension from the college and social security."

"And a few shares of IBM purchased in the forties."

Bea laughed. "You know, she never did cease to amaze me, and she's done it again."

He handed her a copy of the will. "I'll need you to sign a few things in a day or two. It's hard for me to believe you didn't know anything about the bequest."

"She never said a word."

"Unusual. Most people make a thing of it."

"Dr. Bunting was unusual."

"So I've heard." He closed the attaché case and clicked down the tabs. They both stood. Their eyes met again. "I'll call you when the papers are ready."

"At your convenience."

"Unless, of course, we could have lunch tomorrow. The Great Sound Inn is a nice spot."

"That would be pleasant."

"I'll make reservations for tomorrow at one. We can meet there."

"Of course."

"I can find my way out."

The front door clicked open and shut and he was gone. Bea stood in the center of the living room with the will still dangling from her hand. "What have I done?" she asked aloud. During her political career she had often lunched with men other than her husband. She had often gone on trips, either political or during the course of her duties, and she had never questioned her own actions or propriety. This was different. She knew herself well enough to know that she had accepted the invitation for reasons other than business. She had accepted the luncheon date because of an instant physical attraction. She knew it, and she had the feeling that Ramsey McLean knew it as well.

ZEBULON HENDERSON WAS a professional mourner. He had the ability to conjure up genuine tears for the least known of his clients. He maintained a stoic countenance when making the final arrangements with the bereaved family, but during the actual service he held himself erect by the door while silent tears coursed down his cheeks. It gave the family of the loved one a certain sense of identity and place. Lyon had the feeling that if custom or necessity dictated it, Henderson would troop in a full company of mourners and wailers for the proper gnashing of teeth and pulling of hair. He was a man of a different time who was ideally suited for his profession.

Today Zebulon was angry. He sputtered as clawlike fingers pointed to an empty space in the center of the basement room, which was otherwise cluttered with two dozen varieties of coffins.

Rocco Herbert stood patiently with pad in hand until the funeral director managed to regain his composure.

"They came through the back window and then opened the rear door. It was a thirty-five-hundred-dollar deluxe model."

"Any place of business should have an alarm system. EDT would have connected you directly to headquarters."

"This isn't a place of business. We are a social institution. Who'd ever think . . . ? Twenty years in the profession and this is the first time we've ever had this sort of thing happen."

"I think we had better go," Lyon said.

Rocco frowned. "Go where?"

"I think I know where the coffin was taken."

"What in hell are you talking about?"

"There's been one burial in concrete and another under a truck-load of dirt."

"I'll talk to you later." Rocco turned back to Zebulon Henderson. "Now, when was the last time you were down here?"

"Earlier this morning. Around ten."

"I'm serious, Rocco. That coffin is going to be used."

"For God's sake, Lyon! On who?"

"It's even money that Jason Smelts is the candidate."

"You think so?"

"It's a strong possibility."

"Then let's get out of here."

Both men ran up the stairs and out the building. Rocco started the cruiser as Lyon stood indecisively in the center of the empty parking lot. "Come on."

"I suppose you're going to use your siren and drive like a bat out of hell?"

"You know it."

"I'll follow in the truck."

"You drive like an old lady. It'll take you a week to get there. Get in!"

Lyon shook his head and reluctantly slid into the police car. Before the door on his side was shut, they were in the street careening toward the highway. Rocco drove with one hand while the other fumbled for the radio.

"Dispatch. This is M-One. Do you read me?"

"Come in, M-One."

"Call Hartford P.D. Get Sergeant Pasquale for me and have him go to three-seven-three Post Road. Emergency. Tell him I'll meet him there in. . ." He looked at his watch. "Ten minutes."

Ten minutes for a forty-minute drive. Lyon closed his eyes and gripped the seat.

ROCCO WAS wrong. It took them twenty-two minutes to reach Smelts's union headquarters. Pat Pasquale was pacing in front of the building while a uniformed cop leaned against the wall twirling his billy by its leather thong.

When the Murphysville cruiser screeched to a halt behind Pat's unmarked car, Rocco jackknifed from the seat before the vehicle stopped rocking. "Why the hell aren't you in there?"

Pat shrugged. "I think it's called breaking and entering. I don't got a warrant."

"Suspicion of a felony. Rescue of a citizen."

Pat shrugged again. "Far-out guess is the way I look at it. We've had run-ins with these people before." He gestured toward the union logo next to the door. "They'd sue the hell out of us for any infraction."

Lyon spoke in a low, insistent voice. "Two have been killed, Pat. A third man is going to die in that building."

"We busted one of their guys on an assault charge last week. I tell you, Lyon, I can't go breaking in places without more to go on."

Rocco shook his head. "I'm in worse shape than Pat. It isn't even my jurisdiction."

Lyon looked over at the police officer twirling his nightstick.

"Don't look at me, mister. I'm the sergeant's driver, that's all."

Lyon took the club from the officer's hand and advanced to the front door.

"Lovely rainy day, isn't it?" Rocco said as he turned his back to the building.

"If you're a duck," Pat said as he also turned his back.

There was a light mesh across the window in the door, and Lyon inserted the edge of the club under it and pulled the whole panel away. He used the end of the club to break a window and then reached in and unlocked the door. He entered the dim interior of the building. The front vestibule opened into a large meeting room, and he recalled that Jason Smelts's office was in the rear. He bumped into several folding chairs as he made his way to the far end of the building.

The office door behind the podium was locked. He stepped back and ran forward to throw his shoulder against the wood, only to rebound with a painful bruise. He stepped back and shot his foot forward against the panel just below the lock. The wood splintered as the door flew open.

It rested across the desk and was illuminated by a swatch of light that fell through the side window.

It was a dark coffin of highly polished wood.

Lyon pried at the lid and found it to be securely fastened. Other hands were helping as Rocco's fingers tried to find an edge to grasp in order to get more leverage.

"Back away, both of you!" Pat's authoritative voice made them turn. He had a pocketknife in his hand opened to a screwdriver blade. They stepped back as the police sergeant began to work at the screws set into the lid.

Rocco fumbled in his pocket for a coin and began working on

another screw, while Lyon used a letter opener that he found in the top desk drawer.

"I've got a grip," Rocco said and then yelled to the patrolman behind them. "Get the damn lights on!" The officer ran his hands along the darkened wall near the door until they encountered a light switch. Light flooded the room. "Brace the side, Lyon. Pat and I will try to pry the lid off."

Rocco's muscles bulged out as he strained to lift the coffin lid. Lyon braced his feet against the wall behind him and put his shoulder against the box to provide the stability Rocco needed.

"It's coming," Pat yelled.

With a final creaking wrench the coffin lid opened. Lyon's first impression was of the shredded lining and fingernail marks along the inside of the lid's cover.

"Oh." It was a small sound from inside the coffin. "Oh."

"Get him out of there!"

"Oh."

Their hands strained to reach for the man inside the coffin. Rocco put his fingers behind the shoulders and sat Jason Smelts up. Smelts's hands were bleeding from his frantic scratching at the inside of the coffin. His face was bleached white, his eyes were terrified ovals as his chest heaved in frantic gulps. Pat levered the man's legs from the coffin, and with both officers supporting him they lowered Smelts to the floor.

"Are you all right?" Pat asked.

"Oh."

"Respiration seems to be . . . he's hyperventilating," Rocco said. "No evident fractures."

"Oh." Jason Smelts crawled from the grip of the police chief and pushed across the floor into a corner. His hands brushed along the far wall as if searching for a hidden door, and then he curled up in the corner with his feet pulled toward his chest.

"Another few minutes and he would have smothered," Pat said.

"Want me to call an ambulance, Sarge?" The uniformed officer was a short, squat man with a thick neck and coarse features. A name tag on his tunic identified him as Ralston. He looked in fascination at the coffin.

"He seems to be in a state of emotional shock. We'll take him in for a checkup in the squad car."

"Right," the officer responded with his eyes still fixed on the coffin.

"Oh" was the further whimpering sound from the union leader huddled in the corner.

This mass of quivering fear had once sat at his desk behind a waving cigar and defied all authority. Now, he had regressed to some primeval state with his senses numbed in horror. Lyon remembered an incident concerning a South American dictator who used forced burial to break revolutionaries. He would seal his (live) victim in a casket and then suck out the air with a hidden vacuum pump until the prisoner lost consciousness. The unfortunate victim would then be revived and questioned. It was said that not even the strongest held out for more than two turns in the coffin.

"Remember Ti?" Rocco said as he looked at the man cringing in the corner.

"That was a long time ago," Lyon said, but he remembered. Ti had been his ROK interpreter during the Korean War. His zeal in interrogating newly captured prisoners of war had become legendary. Lyon had finally dismissed the man, unable to convince him that a soldier captured in combat was usually in such a state of numbed shock that physical torture was not only immoral, but unnecessary. "Do you think he's physically fit to be questioned?"

"I think so."

"Go watch the front door, Ralston," Pat commanded.

Pat turned to Rocco and said, "Who's going to do it?"

"Wentworth used to be one of the best. And I don't think our friend in the corner needs any strong-arming from me. Go ahead, Lyon."

Lyon sat cross-legged on the floor near the corner. He took the man's clutching fingers into his and squeezed. For an instant he was struck by the incongruity of their present relationship as contrasted to their last meeting in the Clock and Chime. He disregarded the thought and concentrated on the terrified man before him.

"Oh."

"It's all right. You're free. You can't be hurt now." Lyon flexed the man's fingers and felt their grip tighten on his.

"Oh."

Lyon leaned forward until his mouth was only inches from Smelts's. "Someone did this to you. Someone put you in there to die. Who was it?"

"Oh."

"You want to tell me. You want to tell me who put you in there." His voice was a low soothing monotone.

"Yes."

"You entered the office. You saw the coffin on your desk. What happened next?"

"Behind . . . behind the door . . . gun in my back. Made me climb in . . . shut lid . . . couldn't breathe."

"Could you see who it was?"

"Shut lid. No air."

"Could you recognize his voice? Can you tell me who it was?"

"Muffled voice. No air. Tried to get out."

"You have no idea who it was?"

"He's dead. Came back after me. He's dead and wants me dead."

"Marty Rustman?"

"Rustman dead. Buried."

"In the woods. You and Falconer buried him in the woods?"

Lyon felt Pat's hand on his shoulder. He turned to look up at the concerned detective. "You can't go that far without reading him his rights. We won't have a case that will ever hold up in court."

"There's more to it than Rustman." Lyon continued the questioning. "You work for someone."

"Shopton. They have it all. She runs everything."

"What's Shopton?"

"The corporation that controls everything." The concept seemed to click something in the man's frightened mind and part of his fright began to recede. "You . . . must call . . . lawyer."

Lyon stood. "I think that's all I can get. He needs to go to a hospital."

They helped Jason Smelts to his feet and held on to his arms. When he turned toward his desk and again viewed the coffin, his legs buckled. "Oh."

They half-carried him through the door to the waiting police car. Once outside Smelts straightened. He looked past Lyon into some area of horror all his own. "She's responsible! That bitch! That fucking witch! She made me stay here! I could kill her!"

"Okay," Pat said as he helped him into the rear of the car.

"What was that all about?" Rocco asked as the Hartford police car drove off.

"The Truman woman," Lyon said.

8

"WHY DON'T YOU write literature instead of potboilers, Mr. Wentworth?"

All activity on the patio at Nutmeg Hill immediately ceased at the remark. Rocco looked sheepish in his tall chef's hat and emblazoned apron as his barbecue fork froze in midair. His wife, Martha Herbert, flushed, but continued plucking silk strands from husked corn. Bea Wentworth fought back a rising laugh and waited with curiosity for Lyon's response to fourteen-year-old Remley Herbert's remark.

Lyon flipped the marinating flank steak and smiled at the young girl. "I think people write what they can and what they believe in. You like to read those thick historical romances. I don't and therefore couldn't write a very good one. Do you see what I mean? Does that make sense?"

"Yes, it does, but there's not much social significance to your treacly monsters."

"The Wobblies have causes of their own."

"They just seem to run around the countryside with their tongues out. They're not very real."

"I don't think they're supposed to be."

"Remley!" Martha's sharp tone cut across the patio. "Go into the kitchen and make the salad."

"I'm always sent away when we're getting down to basics."

Bea watched the young girl go into the house. "I don't think I got down to basics at her age. She's very precocious."

"Smart-alecky," Martha said. "They wake up the morning they're thirteen and immediately become rotten teen-agers." She plucked an offending strand from an ear of corn.

Lyon flipped the steaks for the final time in the marinade and gathered empty glasses. "Time for one more before the steaks go on."

"I'll have another ice water," Rocco said as he handed Lyon his tall glass.

In the study Lyon stood over the bar cart mixing a martini for Bea, a Manhattan for Martha Herbert, and two double shots of vodka for Rocco's ice water. He poured a pony of sherry for himself.

Bea stood behind her husband as he hummed off-key and deftly mixed drinks. In all the years of their marriage she had never been unfaithful. In fact, she had never considered the possibility. Until today. She had to tell him about Ramsey McLean if only for her own protection. "An attorney named Ramsey McLean came to see me today."

"Oh?"

"He represents the nursing home and was called in to see Faby Bunting. She made a will that left me everything she had."

"I'm sure she felt that you would appreciate her mementos. I think she had some interesting first editions."

"There's money also."

"Donate it to your college library."

"A hundred thousand dollars."

Lyon spilled his sherry. "Are you sure?"

"Ramsey said he'd checked it out in the estate inventory. There's a bunch of old IBM stock that split a dozen times or something."

"I would have thought that all she had was her pension."

"So did I. You still want me to donate it to the college?"

Lyon gave a low laugh. "Did I ever tell you that there's a bit of the hypocrite in me?"

"A teeny bit."

"I think it would be fitting that you give some of the money to the college library as a memorial to Dr. Bunting, but . . ."

"Not all of it?"

"How about we two hypocrites keep half of it?"

"My thoughts exactly."

"By the way, that lawyer from the nursing home, did he mention the Shopton Corporation?"

"There wasn't any way it could come up. By the way, Ramsey is extremely attractive and I'm having lunch with him."

"You probably have to sign something."

"I could have done that in his office."

He handed her a martini and sipped his sherry pensively. "You could find out a couple of things for us at lunch. I'm interested not only in Shopton's interest in the nursing homes, but their other holdings. Any information you could dig up about a woman called Truman would be valuable. Do you suppose you could use your ingratiating ways to find out those things?"

"Yes, Lyon," she said tiredly. "I'll get your information for you, but I don't think you've been listening."

"How's that?"

"I'm having lunch with a very attractive man."

"You've done that dozens of time. Last year at the Democratic National Convention you said you were attracted to Senator Kennedy."

"As a candidate."

"You've always been independent. How is this different?"

Bea sighed. "I guess it isn't." A part of her wanted him to be angry and jealous. He trusted her, and maybe that was the problem.

THE CHAIN SAW whined. Lyon held the vibrating machine in both hands as he looked up at the tree he was cutting. He wondered about its age. Had it been a sapling when Indians roamed the Connecticut River shoreline? Its base was stalwart. A lovely thing. But thirty feet above the ground it branched into a double trunk.

That imperfection marked it as one of the first to be cut down. He pushed the whirring saw deep into the trunk and felt it bite into the wood.

"It's going to fall on the house," the voice behind him said.

"Nope. I've notched it like the book said."

"Have you ever cut down a tree before?" Rocco asked.

"When I was a kid."

"Well, I'm telling you, that thing is going to fall toward the house."

"I read the directions carefully. You can learn to do anything from books."

"Why in hell are you cutting it down? It's a perfectly good tree."

Lyon switched off the chain saw and set it carefully on the ground as he turned to face Rocco. "Are you a cop or a forest ranger?"

Rocco sat on an ancient stump and wiped his brow with a large red handkerchief. "Don't cut that tree down, Lyon."

"I intend to become energy self-sufficient. I've gotten all the appropriate literature from the extension service and discovered that with selective cutting an acre of land will yield a cord of wood a year and never run out. It's self-replenishing. You start by taking out the dead wood, then the sick and old trees like this double-branched one. And we've got over ten acres of timber here."

"I still say you need a block and tackle to pull it away from the house."

"We'll see." He picked up the saw and pulled the cord to kick it to life. "Here goes." The saw cut into the tree as Lyon leaned against it. "What about Smelts?" he yelled over the whine of the saw.

"Pat's trying to build a case on conspiracy, but the prosecutor's not buying it. All we have are hysterical comments he made when we pulled him from the coffin."

"And his laywer marched in and pulled him from your grasp."

"That's about it."

"What about the telephone conversation I overheard between him and the Truman woman?"

"Hearsay evidence. We're still working on it, but right now we don't have Rustman's body or a kidnapping complaint. If Rustman is alive, I don't believe he's in a mood to complain about anyone."

"Here she comes!"

"Only kill them."

"Timber," Rocco said under his breath as the tall tree fell toward Nutmeg Hill. Its top crashed against the living-room bay window and shattered every pane.

Lyon looked disconsolately toward the house and its broken windows. He dropped the saw. "It could have been worse. Luckily Bea always wanted leaded windows in there."

IF SHE WERE TO have imagined a perfect place for an assignation, the Great Sound Inn would probably have been it. It was an unpretentious, rambling old mansion perched on a cliff that protruded into Long Island Sound. Built near the turn of the century for a minor robber baron, it fell into disrepair in the thirties and had been purchased for taxes during World War II. Upstairs there were two dozen airy, light, high-ceilinged rooms overlooking the water, a cozy cocktail lounge tucked away in a corner off the lobby, and a broad expanse of dining room overlooking the sea.

Evidently Ramsey had given her description to the room clerk, for as Bea walked through the lobby toward the dining room, a discreet voice called, "Mrs. Wentworth?"

She turned. "Yes?"

"Mr. McLean is waiting for you in the lounge."

She was ushered into the cocktail lounge. He stood up when she entered and grasped both her hands. "Glad you could come. I bet you're a martini-type lady."

"I am if you wear socks."

"I usually do."

A waiter appeared, disappeared, and reappeared with a stinging-cold vodka martini.

They bantered and laughed and ordered a second drink. The martini tasted better than it should have. She asked the question that shouldn't be asked, not because of its inherent nature, but because it indicated a certain interest on her part. "Are you married?"

"Aren't most people?"

"That's a typical answer."

"That's a typical question."

The martini turned bitter and his warmth cooled. She was disappointed and that shouldn't have been, which told her certain things about her present state of mind that she didn't really care to know. "Of course you're married."

"To an unusual lady named Serena. We have a most interesting marriage in that it's a ménage à trois."

Bea nearly choked on a martini olive. "A what?"

"That's a relationship that is . . ."

"I know what it is. That was a rhetorical what."

"Our ménage à trois consists of me, Serena, and the Dow Jones average."

"She understands the stock market but not you."

"Serena understands all the markets. It's a Truman trait."

"Truman?"

"She wouldn't part with her maiden name. Daddy's last wish or some such. You know, we're practically neighbors. We recently purchased the Yew estate in Murphysville."

"I heard that it had been sold."

"A damn dreary fortress, but Serena likes her privacy."

"I had always thought it might be haunted."

"It is now. We've got the ghost of old man Truman on our shoulders. I think Serena wanted a high-class place for Daddy to haunt."

"And has he?" She had decided that adding a light tone to the conversation would be the safest approach. The chemical attraction between them still existed and operated on a different level than their banter. She wasn't entirely sure she wanted to dispel it.

"Of course. He was a stubborn old bastard. During his lifetime he created a minor financial empire, which he left to his one and only, along with a massive dose of paranoia."

"I can understand how the old place with its walls and isolation could get to anyone." She wondered if talking about one's escort's wife was the best way to stay on neutral ground.

"She's literally turned the damn place into a fortress. We now have guard dogs, metal detectors, and guys on guard that look like the defensive linemen for the Rams. It's not exactly what one would call a cozy domicile."

"Truman," she said again. She had almost missed the connection due to her confused feelings. It was the name that Lyon had asked about.

"As I said, her maiden name once removed. There's a rumor that Daddy changed it somewhere along the line."

"You represent a group of nursing homes for the Shopton Corporation?"

"Yes, among other things."

"Then your wife has an interest in the homes?"

"Controlling interest. Which is probably why she married a lawyer. If she weren't my wife and client, I would call her ruthless. But custom dictates that I refer to her as shrewd."

"You don't sound very happy."

"Perhaps that's why I'm here with you." Their eyes met again. Once again Bea had the same physical reaction she had the first time they met.

"Perhaps we're in the same position," Ramsey continued.

"I've always thought I had a good marriage."

Ramsey took a notebook from the inside pocket of his sport jacket and flipped several pages. "Beatrice Wentworth," he read. "Honors graduate in history. Taught at Murphysville High School until elected to the state house of representatives. Terms in the house and state senate. Chairperson for the Committee on Income Maintenance." He looked up. "That's welfare, isn't it?"

"Yes."

He gave a fey smile. "More?"

"Do you always research your luncheon guests so thoroughly?"

"Only occasionally. I have even more on your husband." He

turned several pages in the notebook and laughed. "Did he really write a book called *The Cat in the Capitol*?"

Bea smiled. "Don't forget *Nancy Goes to Mount Vernon*."

"You have to be kidding?"

"They're for children, naturally."

"I don't see them on the best-seller lists."

"None of them has had spectacular sales, but over the years they stay in print and are consistent sellers. Lyon seems to have a marvelous knack for knowing what children can believe."

"And murder?"

"I beg your pardon."

"Murder . . . You and your husband. My little black book tells me you've been involved in at least half a dozen complex cases."

Bea sipped her cocktail. "It sometimes seems that we attract those cases in some strange way." She looked over the rim of her glass at her companion. "I really can't believe you ran a security check because of our date. In fact, I can't see how you had the time since yesterday to find all that out."

"True. It took several days. At Serena's request, I might add. She's shown a marked interest in your husband's propensity to get involved in murder."

"Why?"

He shrugged. "Who knows? My wife is the sort of person who never approaches a problem in a simple and direct manner. She is the master of circumvention and operates like a Borgia. Let me get your signature on a couple of documents and we'll have that out of the way."

"Fine."

He stood. Their eyes met again. "They're in the car. I'll be right back." He excused himself and slipped from the lounge.

Another drink appeared on the table. The alcohol made the small tremor in her leg disappear. She tested the new drink. It was good, probably the smoothest martini she'd ever had. Obviously he had carefully orchestrated their rendezvous, and she was enjoying it.

She left the table and went to the bar where the bartender was cutting lemon peels into small strips. "Bartender."

He looked at her and a click of recognition registered on his face. "Yes, ma'am?"

"What's in my drink?"

"A martini is made of vodka or gin and a slight touch of dry vermouth."

"Mine isn't vodka or gin."

"Aren't you Senator Wentworth?"

"I am. That is, I'm Bea Wentworth, ex-senator," she smiled automatically.

"I'm from Lincoln in your district. Mae Duckworth's my mother."

"I've known Mae for years. She's a fine woman. Works in the Lincoln Elementary School cafeteria as I remember."

"That's Mom." He looked down at his peels and spoke in a whisper. "That's pure grain in your drink, Senator. One more and you'll walk on the ceiling."

"McLean's private little cocktail?"

"For special guests when I get the signal."

"Always female?"

"Never been otherwise."

Bea felt chilled and cheated. Ramsey's careful set piece meeting had turned sour. He had pressed all the correct buttons and then one too many. She considered his plying her with potent drinks a cheap trick.

McLean returned to the lounge with a thin attaché case. He took out a sheaf of papers and quickly scanned them. Bea left the bartender and returned to the table. She sat across from the attorney and looked at him coolly.

"You have the papers for me to sign?"

"Just two items actually." He passed the documents across the narrow table. "Sign the original and keep the second copy for your personal records."

Bea glanced hastily at the papers and scrawled her signature. She looked up at Ramsey with her most professional smile. "I just received a call from home. My Satureja is sick." She stood. "If you'll excuse me?"

"If it's a . . ."

"An emergency. Yes." Bea left the lounge.

"Hey!" he called after her. "Isn't Satureja an herb?"

So it is, she thought as she left the inn and exited into a strong noon light that hurt her eyes.

It was over and now she wanted to go home.

9

SHE WAS ASLEEP.

He covered her with a light blanket to protect her from the cool river wind blowing through the open window. He switched off the table lamp before he left the room and walked downstairs to the kitchen. He placed a small frozen steak in an iron skillet and ladled leftover salad into a wooden bowl.

Lyon watched the meat sizzle.

Bea had told him about her drinks with Ramsey and the interest Serena Truman had in the Wentworths. Her recounting of the day's events had been concise and dispassionate, and yet, in a certain sense, incomplete. They had often talked over such meetings, and usually he had received an accurate picture of the other person's personality. She had been strangely reticent to talk about Ramsey McLean.

He turned the steak and smiled.

Lyon knew his wife had been tested and had not failed him. He had not been obtuse when she had initially told him about her pending meeting with Ramsey. He was pleased for both of them that her present malaise had not compromised their marriage.

He sat in the breakfast nook and slowly ate the steak and salad.

Now that a possible grave had been discovered and the bloodstains on the rock were determined to be human, the police were convinced that Rustman had somehow survived and was extracting revenge. It was a theory worth considering.

He rinsed his plate and utensils and stuck them in the dishwasher. The muscles in his back tensed as he heard the kitchen-door lock click behind him.

Bea was still asleep upstairs. Only a few people they knew would enter the house unannounced, and he hadn't heard a car in the driveway.

Lyon clenched the skillet handle with both hands and turned with it raised over his head.

A large man in a black suit deftly caught both his wrists and twisted them violently. The skillet fell to the floor and Lyon was pushed back against the kitchen counter. Hands expertly patted his body in a weapon search.

"He's clean," the gravelly voice of his attacker said.

Lyon tried to twist away, but a firm grip kept him pinned against the counter. "Who the hell are you?"

"Tinkerbell."

"Search the house," a woman's voice said.

Lyon's arms were released. The man in the dark suit padded softly up the back stairs. Lyon turned to face a woman holding a small-caliber automatic that was pointed at his midsection.

He judged her to be thirty. She wore a bright red pantsuit that matched her hair. It was nearly the reddest hair he had ever seen, made astonishingly more vivid by its contrast with the albino white of her skin. Slim, arched lines of false eyebrow jutted over deep blue eyes. Her mouth was a thin, narrow line with a touch of lipstick in the same shade as her hair.

She was a striking woman with a touch of the grotesque.

"May I ask the obvious?"

"Serena Truman. I assume you have tea?"

"What?"

"I do hope you have something interesting. I like my tea with a little body."

"Tea? To drink?"

"Of course."

Lyon turned and opened a cupboard. "I do have some Ann Page which has an amusing nuance." He heard a resigned sigh as he turned the flame on under the kettle. He wondered if he should reach for a knife in the utility drawer or run for the phone and dial 911. As long as the lady held the automatic, he didn't seem to have much choice except to try to stay calm and see what developed.

Horace was back in the kitchen. "A dame's asleep in the upstairs bedroom, that's all."

"Thank you, Horace. Wait in the living room so we can talk. Make sure you take the phone off the hook."

"Got it."

Lyon watched the rapid conversation between the unusual-looking woman who so professionally held the small gun and the large man who hovered over her so respectfully. Horace left the kitchen and Serena Truman slipped the safety latch on the automatic and put it back in her shoulder bag.

"I like lemon with my tea, thank you."

"I wouldn't have it otherwise."

When the teapot whistled, he gathered cups, saucers, and spoons while watching Serena Truman from the corner of his eye.

The teapot whistled impatiently and he poured the scalding water over tea bags and set the cups on the table in the breakfast nook. "I don't suppose you've just dropped in for a get-acquainted visit?"

"Do I look like the Welcome Wagon?"

"I'd hate to think what you might be giving away."

"Your wife is having an affair with my husband, Ramsey McLean. In addition to that, someone is trying to kill me."

"My wife is the lady asleep upstairs."

"Who had drinks and games with my husband this afternoon at the Great Sound Inn."

"Drinks, yes. Games, I don't think so."

"You sound ridiculously sure of her faithfulness. What if I were to tell you that I have my husband under constant surveillance?"

"I think you'd be telling a fib."

"I know he took her to the Inn. He has a room there reserved for such times."

"Reservation and occupancy are different."

"He usually gets what he wants."

"He doesn't usually have lunch with Bea."

Her eyes flickered briefly for the first time with a sense of uncertainty. "No matter. It's not even academic at this point. I have already made up my mind concerning my marriage."

"Then that isn't the reason for your visit?"

"No. As I said, I am going to be killed."

"How can you be so certain?"

"Because of this." She handed Lyon a news clipping from a Bridgeport paper.

He read it carefully:

PRODUCE MANAGER FOUND
ASPHYXIATED

Robert Ryland, 41, of 32 Nesbitt Court, manager of the Arcadia Produce Company, was found early this morning by co-workers locked in a refrigerator unit. Company officials conjecture that Ryland inadvertently became trapped in the freezing unit over the weekend. No explanation was given as to how Mr. Ryland became trapped. . . .

Lyon finished the article and placed it carefully on the table between them. "What's your connection with Arcadia Produce?"

"I own it."

"I see." Her eyes and body language portrayed concern. This was a frightened woman who was fighting to retain possession of her faculties. "How does this concern me?"

"You discovered what may have been a grave."

"Your sources of information are excellent."

"You were responsible for saving Smelts."

"I happened to be there."

"Don't be coy, Wentworth. I'm aware of your background. Your involvement in murder cases is well-known to me."

"I write children's books."

"Practically an avocation, it would seem."

"I have, from time to time, inadvertently been involved in certain murder cases."

"And solved them."

"Only when they were thrust upon me."

"Which is why I am here."

"I don't see how . . ."

"I need your help!" She bit the words off and again he detected the hidden traces of fright.

"You have a strange way of asking for it."

She sipped her tea and grimaced at the taste. "I am convinced that someone is going to try to kill me."

"Why don't you explain?"

"My father, who died several years ago, started his career with the Arcadia Produce Company. I suppose you could go beyond that and say he started with a stall at the farmers' market. He was a good businessman, Mr. Wentworth. By the time of his death he had myriad interests."

"The nursing homes, the produce company. Linen supply also?"

"He believed in integrated development."

"Which includes your own labor union."

"Let me just say that we watch Mr. Smelts's union with great interest."

"Everything is interrelated. The nursing homes buy from Arcadia, rent linen from . . ."

"Ajax Linen and Uniform Supply."

"Surely you didn't forget wholesale groceries and meat, and what about hospital supplies?"

"Do you need the names?"

"Not unless they become important."

"All of these deaths by asphyxiation are leading directly to me."

"Do you know why?"

"I run the business, as my father did, with a firm hand. I have made certain enemies along the way."

"Does this firm hand include the kidnapping of Marty Rustman?"

"I am certainly not going to answer that."

"What do you want me to do?"

"Find the killer."

"The police are looking for Rustman."

"And not succeeding. And who's positive that it is Rustman?"

"I have no official capacity."

"That hasn't stopped you before."

"I am not a licensed private investigator."

"Don't play games with me."

"Do what she says, Lyon." Bea, dressed in an old, frayed terry cloth robe, stood in the doorway. "Whoever is killing these people is also directly or indirectly responsible for Fabian Bunting's death. Do what she wants."

Lyon looked from Bea to Serena Truman. "I would say that our interest in these killings is more profound than I realized."

Serena stood up. "Come to my house tomorrow at four. Several of my associates will be present later in the evening."

"At four."

She handed him a small business card with her address and left the house with Horace following.

Lyon let the card fall into the wastebasket. He knew where she lived.

10

THEY SAW THE HOUSE when the car topped the ridge and started down the incline into the valley. The turreted brownstone building seemed to squat between the hills. It dominated the surrounding fields and woods like a feudal castle, but without the warmth of an English manor. It was a bleak house, with high flat walls broken only by an occasional window or small ornamental balcony. A line of yew hedges bracketed the winding drive from the gate. The hedges had been clipped into grotesque gargoyle-like topiary figures.

"My God, look at those hedge figures," Bea said.

" 'Slips of yew, slither'd in the moon's eclipse.' "

"What?"

"The witches' scene in Macbeth. They slipped the guy yew. Got him into all sorts of trouble."

"Oh, the topiary. Well, Ramsey McLean said it was a fortress fit for haunting."

"It must have taken some doing to get those hedges back into shape. The place was vacant for years," Lyon said. "I believe there was some sort of estate dispute. Who's going to haunt it?"

"Serena's father."

"Old Benny. I'm not surprised. He was a mean old curmudgeon."

"You knew him?"

"I checked up on him this morning. They called him the Hartford Strong Man. He just about controlled the wholesale produce market in the entire state. He made a good deal of his money during Prohibition, and God only knows what else he was into."

"Then you didn't buy her pushcart-to-entrepreneur story?"

"If he sold anything from a cart, it was a case of Prohibition Scotch."

"Was he connected to organized crime?"

"He was his own organized crime. Strictly a one-man show. Pat tells a story that the organization from Providence sent over a couple of men to talk with Benny about cutting up percentages. On the following morning they were found dead in an alley with their tongues cut out."

"Sounds like an unpleasant person."

"Serena is his only living child. I wonder how many of his business methods she inherited?"

"Sometimes the second and third generation of dirty money becomes laundered. Do you realize how much of what is now considered old and venerable New England money came from the slave trade?"

"True, but I doubt that Serena has divested herself of the old man's tricks. After all, she is the one who established the phony union and organized its strong-arm tactics."

"I'm still a little vague as to what miracle she expects you to perform, but the day is not a complete loss, since I've always wanted to see the inside of that house."

"She's a very frightened woman. At this juncture, I believe she'd call on the powers of the occult if she thought they could help her. Looking at the way she's had that topiary trimmed, maybe she already has."

A high wall topped with jagged glass shards surrounded the estate and enclosed ten acres of trees, well-tended lawn, and the oppressive yew topiary. A heavy wrought-iron gate was guarded by a large man in a dark business suit who held a shotgun.

"You Wentworth?"

"Yes, I have an appointment."

"Who's she?"

"My wife," Lyon answered.

"Uh huh." The man in the business suit picked up a telephone attached to the wall and spoke in a low tone. He nodded and hung up. "Horace says you can come in. Leave the car outside."

"Not very gracious," Bea said as Lyon parked the Datsun along the edge of the wall. They walked back to the gate, which was now held open by the guard.

A golf cart chugged down the driveway and swung in a half-circle in front of them. Lyon recognized the driver as Serena Truman's companion of the night before. "The big one driving the cart is Horace," he whispered to Bea.

"They both look big," she replied as the first guard swung the gate shut behind them and locked it.

Horace reached from the golf cart and grabbed Bea's pocketbook. He unlatched it and began to paw through the contents.

"Hey!"

Lyon was unceremoniously braced against the wall and frisked for weapons. The two men nodded to each other and motioned to the Wentworths to climb into the golf cart. Horace drove silently up the long driveway.

As they approached a portico, Lyon noticed another guard with a leashed dog pacing along the side of the house. "Has the estate always been an armed camp like this?"

"Only the last few days," the guttural voice replied. The cart swiveled to a stop near the front door. Horace beckoned them to follow.

The door was opened as they approached. The butler who admitted them was a carnival mirror image of Horace. Where Horace was tall and chunky, he was short and thin; where Horace's features were flattened and broad, the butler's were aquiline. They had one thing in common: they both carried shoulder holsters.

Bea and Lyon followed the butler while Horace fell into step behind them. A wide hall bisected the house with various rooms off to either side. Somber portraits of nineteenth-century men and women graced the walls.

"I think the pictures came with the place," Bea whispered to Lyon as she glanced at the portraits.

"Instant family."

They were ushered into a library where Serena Truman sat at an elegant French Provincial table, which had obviously been pushed to the side, away from a direct line with the windows. Horace took an alert, expectant position by the door while the butler disappeared into the interior of the house.

Serena wore a dark blue pantsuit and half glasses that perched on the edge of her nose. She looked over the lenses at them and gestured to two uncomfortable-looking chairs. "You're late."

"The body search at the gate delayed us," Bea said coolly.

"I've had to take a lot of precautions lately."

"Like moving your desk away from the window?"

"There's no sense in tempting a marksman hiding in the hills with a high-powered rifle."

"Your house is very . . . unique," Bea said.

"We haven't had many visitors since we moved in, but tonight will be a unique dinner party. I know you will both find it interesting.

"I'm sure." Lyon wondered what sort of strange guest list this unusual woman had concocted.

Serena closed a file folder containing computer print-out sheets she had been examining and removed her glasses. "Tell me, Mr. Wentworth. Is Marty Rustman alive?"

"We're not sure. Officially he's listed as missing."

"Missing! That could be a euphemism for almost anything." She stood and Lyon was surprised at her height. Although she was not a beautiful woman, there was an inchoate quality about her that hinted at a sublimated sexuality. She walked to the window and stood looking out pensively until she realized where she was standing and rapidly moved away. "I'm afraid to leave here. I'm a virtual prisoner." When she turned to face them, her façade had momentarily fallen away and it was obvious that she was frightened. "It's the way the deaths have occurred that bothers me the most."

"Asphyxiation?"

She looked beyond them toward something invisible to the Wentworths. "Yes. Asphyxiation. I suppose that all of us have one particular terror that frightens us the most, one special way of death that haunts our nightmares."

"And that's yours?"

Her steel veneer slipped further. "Yes, God, yes!" Her retreat was complete, and she now inhabited some long-ago place where she had been as a child. "We once lived in a house on a hill. My brother was two years older and rarely allowed me to play with him. One day he started to build a fort and tunnel into the side of the hill and he let me help. We didn't know about such things, of course. How many children know about shoring and roof supports? It caved in with us inside. We weren't missed for a long while. I remember choking, gasping for breath in the small space left open around me. Finally I lost consciousness, knowing I was dead. The ambulance was there when they finally got me out, and the attendants were able to use the resuscitator. My brother died. Perhaps that was why my father made me into the son he lost." She looked at them blankly until recognition slowly returned to her eyes. "You've got to help me. The dreams have started again."

"You're certainly safe enough here with your guards."

"Am I to live like this for the rest of my life?"

"The authorities will eventually solve the case."

"Eventually could be an eternity for me."

"Mrs. . . ."

"Serena."

"You know that we've found what may be Rustman's grave."

"How can there be a 'may have been' grave?"

"It didn't hold a body."

"Then it's not a grave" was her pragmatic reply.

"It did once."

She made an impatient gesture. "That's no help." She paced the room in masculine strides. Her veneer had fully returned. "I manage rather extensive holdings. In that position I deal in facts, cause and effect, profit and loss. If I apply that same logical system to my present circumstances, I come up with unpleasant answers."

"I'm sure that any costs to your interests will be salvaged when it's over."

"Cost! I'm concerned about my life! People have died who are connected to me. Someone is methodically destroying my operation by murdering my subordinates. I am convinced that I am next."

"I mentioned your security."

She laughed bitterly. "My father would have loved it. I live in a fortress, Wentworth. A prison. As long as I stay hidden away here I am safe."

"Has it occurred to you that keeping you immobile might be beneficial to someone?"

She appraised him with nearly a smile. "Of course. That's why I want you here. You sense these things. I'm well aware that my nursing home executive is about to engage in a proxy fight with my major corporation. It is most beneficial to him that at this critical time I am a prisoner."

"Anyone else?"

"My husband is a philanderer. It is most convenient to him for me to be locked away in this place. Then there is Mr. Smelts who seems to bear me some ill will due to a certain recent confinement of his. But, you shall see them for yourselves. Tonight at dinner you can observe all the leeches."

"I would like to see more of the house," Bea said.

"The full guided tour? Why not?"

They followed her into the hall where Horace, who had been waiting patiently, fell into step behind them. Serena led them through the mansion while commenting more on security arrangements than decor.

"In addition to the gentlemen at the gate, whom you met, we have metal detectors over all the entrances. I believe they're of early-airline-hijacking vintage. The ground floors have some interesting burglar alarms on each window. They produce a rather loud noise if necessary." Her tone had changed to that of a rather bored tour guide in the caverns of a musty cathedral.

There was an antiseptic quality about the rooms that bothered Lyon. The furnishings were obviously expensive and arranged in an orthodox manner, and yet they resembled a decorator's showroom more than a home that was lived in by vital people. He imagined that Serena had had very little to do with the actual decorating.

"How many men do you have on guard?" Bea asked.

"Around-the-clock shifts of six hours each. I feel that eight-hour shifts make men less alert, and alert is how I want them. There is always someone on the gate and another patrolling the grounds with a Doberman. Horace or his counterpart is always near me personally. Other members of the household are armed, exceptionally well paid, and loyal."

"My God, Serena. You have more protection than the President of the United States."

They entered a large living room. Serena walked over to a mahogany dry sink centered unobtrusively along one wall. An iced pitcher of martinis had previously been prepared and a bottle of Dry Sack sherry had been decanted. She poured a cocktail for Bea and sherry for Lyon. Bea noticed that her drink contained an olive. The woman had done her homework well.

Serena raised a glass of Perrier. "To my health. May I have it for the requisite number of years."

Lyon sipped his sherry. The woman standing by the sink fascinated him. He assumed she was a person of some education if the interesting book titles lining the walls in the library were actually read; and yet she was a shrewd and unethical businessperson. It never ceased to amaze him that well-read individuals who had a true appreciation for art and music could still operate in everyday life with ruthless force, with no regard for the basic tenets of human decency.

"I'm not exactly sure what you want Lyon to do," Bea said.

"Merely to observe and draw conclusions from the reactions of people at dinner tonight. I have approached the problem as I would any other and planned my assault accordingly. Those I have invited here tonight have strong motives for killing me. I am going to add to their discomfort with certain disclosures."

"Such as?"

"We have already spoken about Gustav Tanner and his un-bridled ambition. He will be informed that I am not only aware of his attempts to pick up voting rights in Shopton, but he will be told that I have circumvented his efforts. His services will be terminated at once."

"If he doesn't have a motive when he arrives here, he will when he leaves," Bea said.

"My husband, who wants the security of marriage to my money along with the sexual license of a college boy, will be informed of our imminent separation. Needless to say, the legal documents will be drawn by my new law firm."

"It doesn't sound like the type of dinner party I'd prefer," Bea said under her breath.

"Mr. Smelts will be asked to resign from the union due to ill health. Which, if he doesn't comply, he will certainly have. We are going to be under pressure in that area soon, and I would just as soon that he took the fall."

"He blames you for what happened to him in his office."

"Mr. Smelts always blames others for his own stupidity. His inefficiency will no longer be tolerated."

"Who else is going to be at this happy gathering?"

"Marty Rustman's wife. I am most interested in her reaction when I tell her that her husband is alive and aware of her bedding down with Mr. Tanner."

"Marty may not be alive."

"It doesn't matter as far as my remarks are concerned. What will matter is how Mrs. Rustman reacts. That is what you will watch, Mr. Wentworth. I will expect your conclusions later."

"I told you that I am not . . ."

"I know exactly what you are and what you have done. That is why you are here."

"I think you have been given a royal command, Lyon," Bea said. "And I think it's time for us to go home."

"We'll stay," Lyon replied quietly and put his hand over Bea's.

"I have arranged for the personnel and other files of all my interests to be brought here. I would like you to review them for any further possibilities I may have missed. I pay well, by the way."

"I can't accept money."

She smiled crookedly. "Everyone has a price. We'll discuss that aspect later."

"I will look at the files. It would be helpful also to have the union files here."

"That has been arranged. Mr. Smelts has seen fit to loan them to me."

"How convenient," Bea muttered.

"As I said. The files are in the study. Cocktails will be served at seven, dinner at eight. The other guests will arrive at seven."

LYON SAT AT THE French Provincial table in the study surrounded by folders. He could see a guard outside walking back and forth along the side of the house. His Wobblies sat on the edge of the windowsill. Their tongues lolled to the side as they watched.

The Ferret in the Fortress. Maybe not a bad idea. He would set the book in an interesting historical period, perhaps during the early Crusades. Richard Lion-Heart would be the leader of a band that . . .

"Lyon."

"Huh?" He returned to reality to look at Bea.

"What do you think of her?"

"I think she's a piranha."

"Then why did you agree to stay and participate in this charade?"

He thought for a moment. "Because she may be right and because it intrigues me."

"The deaths of Maginacolda and Falconer were not any great loss to society."

"There's also the man in the produce company that we don't know anything about, Marty Rustman, and Fabian Bunting."

"So we stay."

"Have you looked at the union files?"

"I'm doing it now."

"I would imagine there might be enough there to show illegal connections."

"Enough so that I can file a complaint with the state labor commissioner in the morning. I'm surprised that she's so willing to reveal them to us."

"You're being used."

"How's that?"

"She's letting us see the files because she knows that you will file a complaint. Then Smelts gets hung. She's a survivor, Bea. As she said, she'll let Smelts take the fall and extricate herself. I'd be very surprised if you found anything that had a direct connection to Serena."

THE SUN FELL behind the estate walls throwing shadows of elongated trees across the grounds. Lyon looked up from his study of the files, rubbed the bridge of his nose, and sat looking across the darkening yard.

A phone rang somewhere.

Bea was working at his side. She had filled a dozen pages on a yellow legal pad with names, facts, and dates. Lines crisscrossed from one name to another in a confusing maze.

"Find out anything?"

"Enough to delight Kim and destroy that rotten union."

"I recognize a few of the guards we've seen."

"From where?"

"They are men I met in Smelts's office one night."

A voice from behind them at the doorway startled them. "Cocktails are served in the living room."

"Is that an invitation or an order?" Bea asked.

Lyon put the files aside neatly. "Serena said we'd find it interesting. Shall we go?"

"Of course, sir." They linked arms and walked down the hall toward the living room. They could hear the low murmur of voices and the clink of ice in glasses. They paused at the archway leading into the room. "You said interesting, I'd say incongruous."

"Agreed."

The butler stood before them with a tray holding a sherry for Lyon and a martini for Bea. They automatically took the drinks.

Barbara Rustman was in a corner talking to Gustav Tanner. The hospital administrator spoke softly into her ear and she shook her head violently.

Jason Smelts was in a conspiratorial conversation with Ramsey McLean on the sofa. He punctuated his remarks by slamming a fist into a palm. Ramsey saw them and left the protesting labor leader with relief. He shook Lyon's hand and held Bea's a moment too long until she withdrew it from his grasp.

"I wasn't sure you'd be here."

"I think we are here by edict," Lyon said.

He laughed. "Serena doesn't believe in social niceties."

"She seems to meet problems head-on."

"My wife is one for militarylike protection of her vulnerable areas."

"Do you know why everyone is here?"

"I've guessed. You, the Wentworths, are here as her insurance. I don't know if she's told you or not, but Serena is convinced that everyone here has a motive to kill her."

"Do they?"

"Mr. Smelts just told me he has. He knows he's going to be tossed to the wolves. In fact, he feels he already has been placed in jeopardy."

"Tanner?"

"I handled that for Serena myself. Tanner will make his move at the annual meeting and be cut to ribbons."

"Do you exclude yourself?" Bea asked.

"Of course not. Please, excuse me, I have to check with the cook on dinner arrangements."

"Cynical, isn't he?" Lyon said when Ramsey left.

"I'm finding him less and less attractive."

Jason Smelts approached them warily. "What in hell are you doing here, Wentworth?"

"I'm a guest. How are you feeling?"

"Lousy. Seeing you here doesn't help my disposition."

Lyon saw Bea's shoulders straighten. It was a sign he knew well. His wife was preparing for battle. "You seemed only too glad to see Lyon when you were suffocating in your office."

"What's that supposed to mean?"

"Your gratitude is boundless," Bea said.

Smelts's face reddened. "Who the hell is this broad?" He gulped the remainder of his drink.

"My wife."

Smelts faced Bea and rattled his ice cubes near her face. "I know who you are. Christ! You're that pinko, bleeding-heart politician who's either sucking up to the welfare cheats or the bull dykes."

"Don't confuse feminism with sexual predilection, Mr. Smelts."

"Same thing."

"I think not."

The clinking ice cubes wavered toward Lyon as if shaken by some aboriginal shaman. "If you kept her knocked up, she'd stay home and out of trouble."

Lyon felt a sudden surge of anger. "We're both rather disturbed about your union's interesting arrangement with the Shopton Corporation."

"You don't know from nothing."

"We spent a cozy afternoon with your files," Bea said.

Smelts grabbed the sleeve of the passing butler and rattled his ice cubes under the surprised man's nose. "Get me another one." He turned back to the Wentworths. "She's setting me up, isn't she?"

"Have you always been a corrupt labor leader?" Bea asked. "Or is this only the latest of a series of cons?"

Lyon knew that Bea was off and running. He'd seen her take up the cudgels before; he had seen her joust with other enemies. Smelts represented the type of corruption of trust she hated the most. He knew his wife would plunge forward without regard to the very real physical danger Jason Smelts represented.

"I don't care for the question," Smelts replied slowly to Lyon.

"You can speak directly to me, Mr. Smelts. I am a grown-up lady."

"What's Serena been telling you?"

"More than enough to interest the Labor Department and possibly a grand jury. A complete audit of the pension fund should make interesting reading." Bea's anger at the man overcame her natural reluctance to be Serena's tool in his destruction.

"The bylaws say I can invest those funds any way I see fit."

"I think the law calls it Larceny at Trust."

"I don't have to answer that."

"Not to me, you don't."

Three men moved simultaneously: Smelts lunged toward Bea as Lyon placed himself between them, while Ramsey McLean put a restraining hand on the labor leader's shoulder.

Smelts tried to wrench away from McLean's grip as he glared at Bea over Lyon's shoulder. "I could . . ."

"As your attorney," McLean interjected, "I advise you not to say one more word."

Smelts hesitated and then turned brusquely away and walked over to the butler for his drink.

"He can be dangerous," Mclean said. "I wouldn't pursue it any further with him tonight."

Smelts obtained his drink and stalked back toward them. He pushed McLean's protesting palm aside. He addressed himself to Bea. "You know, you ask dumb questions. You think that when a guy's young he goes around saying, 'Gee, I'm going to grow up to be a corrupt labor leader.' It don't happen that way. You start out as a worker. You get maybe to be shop steward. One day you find somebody palming you a five for looking the other way. If you got any brains you grow outa the nickel-and-dime stuff and hold back until they meet your price. You got that, lady! You hear me? And I'll swear I never said it."

"That's enough, Smelts," McLean said.

"You tell Serena that I'm not taking the fall." Jason Smelts walked away from them to the far side of the room.

"On edge, isn't he?"

"He has a right to be. You heard what happened in his office?"

"I was there."

"I would say that would be enough to unnerve any man. His thinking hasn't been right since."

Barbara Rustman plucked at Bea's sleeve and the two women walked over to sit on a settee. "How are you, Barbara?"

"Do you know why I was asked here, Mrs. Wentworth?"

"How were you invited?"

"This large man came to the house and insisted that I come."

"I think Mrs. Truman wants to talk to you about Marty."

"I'm not sure he'd like that. Unless he's dead. Do you think he's dead?"

"I don't really know."

Lyon watched the clusters of people interspersed throughout the large room. There was a conspiratorial air to their intimate conversations. He wondered what reactions Serena hoped to get later in the evening. In a corner, Ramsey McLean finished dialing the phone and beckoned to him.

"Any messages for McLean? . . . Thank you." He hung up and turned to Lyon. "Out of curiosity, Wentworth, in that material my wife gave you this afternoon, was there anything pertaining to me?"

"No, there wasn't."

The phone near McLean's elbow rang three times before Ramsey picked up the receiver. His words were clipped and annoyed. "Yes . . . it's nearly eight and we're ready to eat. . . . I understand." He slammed the phone down. "Serena overslept. She'll be late for dinner. She wants us to go ahead and start. Frankly, I think she enjoys being late in order to make the grand entrance."

"I'm surprised she didn't arrange for Marty Rustman to make an appearance."

"Even her power doesn't reach to that great union hall in the sky."

"Then he's dead?"

"I don't know."

"If he is alive, what interest would he have in Serena?"

"Are you that naïve?"

"Then she ordered his kidnapping?"

"You said it, Wentworth. I didn't."

"Isn't that an expensive way to dispose of a recalcitrant labor leader?"

"We lawyers love hypothetical situations, so let me indulge myself. Let us assume that Rustman had proof about the relationship between Smelts and the corporation."

"That would require his disposal."

"Hypothetically it might."

"You are aware that my wife has enough information to go to the Labor Department?"

"Yes."

"Then what happens to Smelts?"

"The decision has been made to disband the union. Its functions have become more trouble than they are worth."

"And when charges are brought?"

"To quote one of my favorite Machiavellian people, 'We'll watch him slowly twist in the wind.' "

"Smelts feels he's already twisted."

"That's a risk Serena was willing to take. Serena is always protected." He made an expansive gesture around the room. "As this house proves."

"It's almost pathological."

"Of course. Serena is crazy."

"Dinner is served" was the call from the unobtrusive butler in the hallway.

Bea held on to Lyon's arm as everyone else straggled from the room toward the dining room at the end of the hall. "Will you tell me what kind of game is going on here?"

"I'm not sure, but it is interesting. You have to admit that."

They were the first to arrive at the dining room. It was a long room with heavy, dark wooden paneling that gave it an oppressive aura. Table settings bracketed by heavy silver bowls were interspersed along the table. Small hand-lettered cards identified the places. Lyon and Bea were seated together. Barbara Rustman entered next, nodded in a shy way, and then stood by a chair at the opposite side of the table.

Jason Smelts and Gustav Tanner entered separately and were followed shortly by Ramsey McLean.

"Please sit down, everyone. Serena will be along in a moment."

It was a quiet meal served by the silent butler. It appeared to Lyon that they had been purposely seated some distance from each other in order to destroy any possible sense of intimacy. Ramsey was at one end of the table, while the place at the far end was conspicuously vacant.

It was during the entrée that Horace entered and whispered something in Ramsey's ear. Ramsey stood up and neatly folded his napkin. "If you will excuse me a minute? Something seems to have delayed my wife. Mr. Wentworth, will you please accompany me?"

Bea shot Lyon a quick glance as he followed Ramsey into the hall and toward the main stairwell.

"What seems to be the difficulty?" Lyon asked as they followed Horace to the second floor.

"I'm not sure. Horace has been on guard outside Serena's room. Something has happened that makes him concerned."

They were led down the hallway and stopped before a door where a straight-backed chair was placed against a nearby wall. Lyon conjectured that this was where the bodyguard sat while Serena was in her room.

A small trickle of water flowed through the slight crack between the door and the floorboards. Ramsey glanced at Horace. "Well?"

"A few minutes ago I heard her run water in the bathtub. Then . . . look." He pointed toward the trickle of water seeping over the hall carpeting.

"Serena!" Ramsey pounded on the door. "Serena! Are you all right!" He pressed his ear against the door. "I can hear water running."

"I think you had better go in," Lyon said.

"Do you have a key, Horace?"

"No, sir. She locks it from the inside."

"Serena!" Ramsey pounded on the heavy wooden door again. "Answer me!"

"Break it in," Lyon said to Horace.

The large bodyguard nodded, looked at Ramsey for permission, and then threw his shoulder against the door. He bounced painfully back into the center of the hall. "Solid as hell."

"Get a crowbar or something from wherever the tools are kept."

"Yes, sir." Horace moved quickly down the hall toward the stairwell.

Lyon knelt and felt the seeping water with his finger. "Where's the bath?"

"It's located right against the hall wall."

"This water is warm."

"What in hell's going on?"

Horace ran back down the hall followed by another man carrying a shotgun at port arms. The bodyguard held a hammer and chisel and stooped before the locked door and jammed the chisel between the frame and the panel. Hammer blow after hammer blow struck against the chisel as he separated a hinge from the door. When he was satisfied, he threw his bulk against the panel. The frame splintered as the door flew backward to slam against the wall.

A thin film of water covered much of the entranceway flooring and was seeping out the door into the hall.

Ramsey went into the bathroom and immediately stepped back into the hall. "Oh, my God!"

Lyon went into the steam-filled room. The sunken tub's rushing hot water faucet filled the room with clouds of moisture-laden warm air.

The nude woman in the tub with the plastic bag tied over her head stared through the steam with unseeing eyes.

11

LYON HAD SEEN IT too often before. The caretakers of death were uniformed and efficient. They overflowed the room: police, ambulance attendants, the assistant medical examiner in a rumpled sport coat with leather patches on the elbows, and a tired Rocco Herbert.

Lyon stood in the hallway leaning against the wall. He had spoken briefly to Bea, and she had remained downstairs with the others. Ramsey McLean was giving a statement to Jamie Martin further down the hall, while in the murder room Rocco gave directions to a police photographer.

Nothing changed.

The water overflowing the tub had been turned off, but the body wouldn't be disturbed until pictures were taken and the doctor had made his initial inspection.

It was apparent without a medical examination that she had died from suffocation—the death she feared most. Her distorted, fearful features imprisoned inside the transparent bag were more than Lyon cared to remember.

The photographer finished taking his last shot and stepped away from the tub. His place was taken by the medical examiner who bent toward the body. Rocco motioned to Lyon with a cocked finger.

"I'd like you to look."

"I already have."

"We're about ready to move the body."

Lyon didn't want to see it again. Probably the last thing in the world he cared to view again was the terror on Serena Truman's face. Rocco motioned again and Lyon stepped into the bedroom and looked into the bath.

The steam had cleared. Mud from police shoes streaked the tile floor. Serena was the same. The same as she would always be.

"Her hands are tied with a short belt," Rocco said. "It looks like it matches a dress in her closet."

"Time of death?"

"Impossible to tell exactly," the medical examiner snapped. "The hot water has kept the body temperature from falling. I may be able to tell something when I get her on the table and examine the contents of the stomach, but it won't be accurate."

"A ball-park guess?" Rocco asked.

"When was she discovered?"

"A little after eight."

"When was she last seen?"

"We're not sure until we talk to everyone else, but Lyon saw her at five."

"The guard at the door tells me he heard her in here a little after eight."

"Then you got it," the medical examiner said. "Eight or a few minutes after."

Rocco signaled to the medics standing in the hall. "You can have it."

Lyon turned away from the bathroom and walked slowly through the bedroom. It was a spacious room with a large king-sized, canopied bed along one wall. The far side of the room had been converted into a sitting area and contained a chaise longue, two easy chairs, and a desk. A dressing table, two bureaus, and a large walk-in closet with mirrored doors completed the furnishings.

An officer was dusting furniture for prints. The bagged body was trundled from the bathroom and down the hall.

Bedding had been turned down on one side of the bed and a pillow was indented. An open book lay facedown on the far side of the bed. Lyon bent to read the title, *Creative Management*. Silk pajamas lay in a heap by the side of the bed. They looked as if they had been carelessly dropped rather than stripped from the woman who had once worn them. There was a lamp and telephone on a night table.

The room seemed undisturbed. A hostess gown with underthings and accessories was laid out neatly on the chaise longue. One of the large closet doors was partially ajar, but otherwise the clothing hung in neat lines. There was an open jewelry box on the dressing table with a diamond necklace on the tabletop. He bent over the necklace and saw that the setting contained more than a dozen diamonds of obvious quality.

"That thing's worth a bundle," Rocco said from behind him. "It would be easy as hell for any burglar to rip the diamonds from the setting and fence them."

"Anything missing?"

"Not that we can tell. We'll do an inventory and talk to the hired help to make sure. My guess is that nothing's gone."

"Then it's not robbery?"

"If it was, it would be the first burglar in my experience who tied a bag over the victim's head and left a necklace like that."

"Perhaps whoever put the bag on her didn't intend to kill her, but only meant to keep her quiet."

"You saw the look on her face. Do you believe that?"

"No." Lyon walked over to large French doors. He used his elbow to unlock the latch and push them open. They led to a narrow balcony that was obviously more ornamental than functional. He looked over the side of the building. It was a sheer drop of thirty feet. "Earlier there was a guard in the yard on this side of the building."

"Dumb bastard was still marching back and forth like a tin soldier when we arrived. A big guy carrying a loaded twelve gauge shotgun. We called him inside for a statement."

"Why don't we talk to the guard who was outside the bedroom door?"

"My idea exactly." Rocco turned to Jamie Martin standing in the hall. "Get Horace in here."

Horace looked devastated when he entered the bedroom. Lyon recalled a tight television shot of a defensive football lineman after the loss of a close game. Horace looked like he had lost a dozen close games.

Rocco flipped a pad from his breast pocket. "Name?"

"Horace Mandel."

"You worked for Serena Truman?"

"I was her aide."

"Aide?" Rocco looked up from his notes. "Aide? Now, Horace."

"Guard. I used to work for one of the nursing homes, but she called me in to watch over her. She was worried someone was going to waste her. I guess she was right, wasn't she?"

"You were on guard at the door?"

"From the time she came in here until just now when she left in the bag."

"Anyone come in or out?"

"No one. I swear to God. No one. And I didn't leave the door for one minute."

"To have a smoke? To go to the john? Not a minute?"

"Not a second, except for when I went to get Mr. McLean at dinner."

"And the door was locked?"

"From the inside."

"I'll vouch for that," Lyon said. "We had to break it in."

Rocco looked unhappy. He often did when faced with seemingly insurmountable problems. "All right, Horace. You're telling me that you were on guard in the hallway at the only entrance to this room, and that there was also a guard in the side yard under the window?"

"That's the way we set it up for security reasons."

"Tell me what happened."

"That's it, goddamnit! Nothing happened."

"You knew something was wrong. You were worried enough to go downstairs and get Mr. McLean."

"She came in here for a nap like she always did before dinner. Miz Truman didn't drink. If they were having people in for cocktails, she would wait up here until dinner was served. I saw her getting ready for bed when I closed the door. She locked it from the inside. That was just after five."

"Then what?"

"I keep telling you. Nothing."

"At eight?"

"I heard her start the water in the tub. The pipes are in the wall near the hall and they're old. They gurgle and make noise, you know."

"What time?"

"Just after eight. The water kept running and running until in a while I saw some dribbling under the door. The tub ran over, you know."

"That's when you went to get Mr. McLean?"

"Right. We had to break the door down. You know the rest."

"I'll talk to you later for a formal statement. Go downstairs and stay with the others. Send up the guard who was outside the house."

Horace left without a word. They heard him lumbering down the hall muttering under his breath. Rocco's face was creased with questions. "How in hell did the son of a bitch who did this get in here?"

"This is a strange house."

"I hope you're not suggesting we sound all the walls and move the furniture to find some goddamn hidden entrance?"

"I don't think you'll find one, but you had better try."

"I have the guard who was outside the window," Jamie Martin said from the doorway.

"You heard what happened," Rocco said to the guard.

"You know it."

"Did you see anything?"

"Not a damn thing."

"When did you take your post outside the window?"

"A few minutes before eight. That's when we usually change shifts. All of us, that is, except Horace."

"You didn't hear or see anything?"

"Nothing. I noticed her light go on, that's all."

"When was that?"

"A couple a minutes after I came on duty. I took my post before eight, and when I was standing under the window, I saw the light flick on."

"Anything else?"

"Naw. Except that Kurt is missing."

"Who the hell is Kurt?"

"A guard dog. He was supposed to be turned over to me by the guy I took over from. He wasn't there. They said he ran off and that was the last they saw of him."

"Okay, we'll get your formal statement later. Stick around." The fingerprint man finished and left with the outside guard. "Well?"

"You've got a problem on your hands."

"Which means that the first order of business is to find out who of that bunch downstairs was missing at eight."

"No one was," Lyon answered. "We were all in the living room having drinks. We all saw Ramsey answer the phone when Serena called."

"You're sure of that?"

"Verify it independently with Bea and the others."

"I'll get statements from everyone. Right now my large Italian-Irish nose points toward Horace. He was the one sitting outside the door when the homicide occurred." Rocco left.

Lyon sat on the edge of the bed and stared at the wall. If he were a superstitious man, he might believe in emanations from the dead. Something intangible filled the room with the stench of death. He knew, rationally, that it was his own psychological creation, but he couldn't shake the feeling that gripped him.

She hadn't been a very nice person. She had pursued power and wealth without compassion, but she had died a horrible death. They all had. From Bunting to Serena, the chain of bizarre murders had been brutal.

He lay back on the bed and closed his eyes. There must be a pattern. There had to be direction behind what appeared to be random events.

The Wobblies perched on the balcony parapet and looked at him with red eyes.

"Easy enough for you guys to get up there, but how about a man?"

They often didn't answer if they didn't have much to say.

"What do you guys think about all this?"

"Get off the evidence."

It wasn't like the Wobblies to talk like that.

"Damn it all, Lyon! We've got to seal off this room, and I don't want to seal you in it."

Lyon's eyes blinked open to see Rocco hovering over the bed. "Oh, sorry." He swung his feet to the floor and noticed that the Wobblies had fled. "Find out anything?"

"Sure. I found out that you guys were all belting down drinks when the lady was murdered."

"Then you're positive of the time sequence?"

Rocco looked tired. "Several people verify the time Ramsey McLean received a phone call from Serena as eight or near eight. The guard outside had just come on duty when the light came on, and that was eight. Horace, outside the door, if you can believe him, and we seem to have corroboration, heard the water."

"At eight."

"You've got it."

"Which seems to rule out everyone who was downstairs having drinks."

"But not ol' Horace."

Lyon walked to the shattered bedroom door and bent to examine the lock. "The key's still in the lock. From the inside."

"He might still have opened it from the outside."

"Not this door. Come take a look."

Rocco bent over the lock. It was an old, square affair with a large key inserted from the inside. A key inserted from the outside could not possibly move the tumblers without dislodging the inside key. "Great."

"Which would seem to mean that from eight until a very few minutes after eight, someone had to gain entrance into this room."

"Without passing a guard in the hall or being seen by the guard outside."

"And in that short time span he or she had to kill Serena and manage to escape undetected."

"The only person in this whole affair who has managed to pull off disappearing tricks like that is Marty Rustman."

"He's not superhuman, Rocco."

"You'll want to hear the statements and tour the grounds."

"I want to go home and go to bed. You can fill me in tomorrow."

"I'll probably be here until then."

LYON AWOKE TO SEE streaks of pink across the sky outside the window. Some unusual noise had penetrated his subconscious and awakened him. The house was now silent with the quiet of early dawn.

When it started again, he immediately recognized the sound.

Bea sat bolt upright in bed. "Someone's in the house."

"It's my typewriter in the study."

"Does she have to start so early?"

"Since we've been gone so much lately, I gave her a key." He slipped on his robe and slippers and walked downstairs. Mandy Summers was bent over his manuscript trying to decipher a marginal note. "Good morning."

She whirled the desk chair to face him. Her body arched in fright as her hands reached up to ward off a blow. "Mr. Wentworth. I didn't hear you come downstairs."

"I'm sorry I startled you." He wondered how deep the fear ran in this woman. "Would you like coffee?"

"That would be nice. I couldn't sleep so I thought I'd get an early start. I hope that's all right?"

"As I said when you started, do it at your own pace." He turned to leave.

"I don't sleep well. I always see him when I'm alone at night. It's as if he were still here coming after me."

"He's not here, Mandy. I'll put coffee on."

He found Bea in the kitchen with the coffee pot already perking. She poured two glasses of juice and they sat in the breakfast nook.

"I assume that's Mandy in the study?"

"She doesn't sleep well."

"That woman is held together by very thin wires."

"I know, but I don't see what more we can do for her."

A car pulled into the driveway. Bea leaned toward the window and pushed aside the curtain. "It's Rocco. He looks terrible."

Lyon opened the back door and the police chief pushed grumpily past him. "I see some of us got some sleep last night," he said as he glared at Lyon's robe.

"You've been out there all night?"

"Every blessed minute of it. I had the state lab boys to keep me company. Got any coffee?"

"Good morning, Chief Herbert," Bea said with a warm smile.

Rocco slouched into the breakfast nook and accepted coffee with a grateful smile. "I saw your light on from the road."

"We're always up at five A.M. It builds character."

"Want to hear what we found?"

Lyon poured coffee, took a sip, and then leaned back on the bench with his hands laced behind his head as he stared at the ceiling. It needed painting, but he would try to ignore that. "All you have."

"As a special favor the ME went ahead and did the autopsy last night. It's definitely death by asphyxiation."

"Time?"

"He couldn't be conclusive. She died anywhere between five and eight. She ate an extremely light lunch, perhaps nothing at all, so there was little in the stomach that would allow him to pinpoint the time. You already know that her immersion in hot water made body temperature a poor indicator of when she expired. We've officially set the time of death at between eight-o-five and eight-ten due to the other corroborative evidence."

"By that I imagine you mean the running water, the light turning on, and the phone call?"

"You can't get more conclusive than three separate indicators. We're also sure that during that time span, you, Bea, Tanner, Smelts, Barbara Rustman, and McLean were either finishing drinks in the living room or in the dining room."

"Which rules out everyone but the guards."

"Not necessarily."

Lyon leaned forward. "Oh?"

"We've discovered three important pieces of evidence. The guard dog that ran off was found poisoned in the woods near the wall. We also found fiber threads on the top of the wall near where the dog was killed. There are fresh footprints on either side of the wall. The guards claim they hadn't been near that particular area in several days. I think Rustman climbed the wall, killed the dog, and was able to gain entrance into the house."

"And how did he get into the murder room?"

"We haven't figured that one out yet. Any more of that coffee, Bea?"

"You searched the room again?"

"We even drove steel spikes into the walls. That house is built like a brick sh . . . fortress. The walls are two feet thick and there's no means of access to that bedroom except through the French doors at the balcony or the hall door."

"The bedroom door to the hall was locked from the inside and the French doors were latched from the inside. How do you reconstruct it from what you have?"

"We feel there are two possibilities: Rustman got inside the house, somehow entered the room, surprised Serena in the tub, and killed her; or it's one or more of the guards. They all have records for assault and would sell their sisters to a massage parlor for a buck and a half."

"If it was the guards, why would they poison the dog and leave fibers on the wall?" Bea asked.

"To point suspicion at Rustman."

"Motive."

"Paid off. Everyone invited to that dinner party had a strong motive to kill Serena. Any one of them could have bribed one or more of the guards."

"Well, thanks," Bea said.

"Present company excluded. Either that, or Rustman survived his kidnapping and has been working his way up the corporation to Serena."

"Killing people by asphyxiation along the way."

"And there's no word on where he is?"

"We still have the APB out for him, and we've searched every known haunt and staked them out . . . not a sign."

"And maybe there's another alternative."

"Like what?"

"I'm not sure. Except we can't tell anything until we know how the killer got in and out of that room. Is anyone out at the estate?"

"McLean's at a hotel in Hartford, and I have the house sealed off and guarded."

"I think I'd like to go out there."

"I'll radio and tell them you're coming. I'm going home to bed."

12

"WHY ARE WE doing this?"

Lyon's arm rested in the open window as he drove toward the Truman house with nonchalant ease and at a moderate speed. "What do you mean?"

"Well, we're all pretty much agreed that Dr. Bunting was killed by Maginacolda."

"Most likely."

"Then we should be out of it. Good Lord, Rocco's got almost all his men on the case and now the state police are involved. Which means there's no reason for us to look at any crime scenes."

"We're involved because Rocco wants us to be."

"You know, Wentworth, you don't fool me a bit. There's a part of you that enjoys this, that relishes this break in your routine. Why don't you take a vacation between books like other writers?"

Lyon looked over the hills that gently sloped down toward the valley where the Truman house rested. The upper stories of the house were now visible over the wall. He wanted to articulate his thoughts to his wife, but knew they must come out without pomposity, a quality she detested.

"I don't suppose Serena Truman was my prime candidate for a favorite person."

"Nor the others."

"Certainly not Maginacolda and Falconer."

"And you think those killings are related?"

"I think the telephone call I heard Smelts make to Serena places the ultimate responsibility for Rustman's kidnapping with her."

"Which leads back to the fact that Rustman is alive and active."

"Maybe."

"Oh, I hate it when you're cryptic."

"I don't have the answers yet."

"Then drive on, MacDuff."

"In answer to your other question, I guess there is a part of me that's fascinated with murder. It's the ultimate crime and I'm obsessed by it."

"Where do we start?"

"At the wall where they found the fabric fibers."

Rocco had told Lyon that the fibers were found on the northerly wall, approximately 150 yards from the road. Lyon parked the Datsun up from the gate and began to pace off the yardage. He stopped at the appropriate distance and stepped back from the wall. "How tall was Rustman?"

"Five seven."

"He'd have a hell of a time getting over the wall. If he had jumped and caught the edge, his hands would have been cut on the glass embedded on top and there would have been traces of blood."

"Nope."

"Idea?"

"Uh huh." Bea walked briskly back to the car, got behind the wheel, and started the vehicle. She drove parallel to the wall and stopped near where Lyon stood. She left the car, climbed onto the hood and then onto the roof. Her head and shoulders were now above the wall. She looked down at Lyon. "I'm as tall as Rustman. Are there tire marks down there?"

He bent to examine the soft ground. "Yes. Not far from the plaster cast molds that Rocco made of the footprints."

"Want me to go over the wall and leave some fiber from my derrière on the glass?"

"I'll take your word you could do it. In the meantime, you're denting the car roof."

Bea climbed down. "It's possible then?"

"Sure. But what about getting out again?"

"He didn't come out this way. There're plenty of places to hide on the grounds. Weren't the guards called to the house when the police arrived?"

"I believe they were. He could have hidden and then just walked out."

"It's possible."

They got back into the car, backed down the wall to the road, and drove to the gate. A uniformed cop was inside the gate, leaning against his car reading a paperback western. As their car approached, he looked up in annoyance until he recognized Lyon. "The chief said you'd be coming, Mr. Wentworth." He opened the gate and they drove through.

"Now what?" Bea asked.

"We're not going to make any forward momentum on this case until we discover how Serena was killed. At that point we might be able to fill in the missing pieces."

They parked by the front door and Lyon took a penciled diagram from his pocket. He examined it for a few moments.

"Lead on," Bea said.

"I think we should start at the spot where the dead dog was found."

They walked around the side of the house toward Serena's window before turning at a right angle toward the wall. The body of the dead animal had been found twenty yards from the wall on a direct line with the murder-room window. The spot was near where the clothing fibers had been found, but it was obscured from the house by trees. Lyon stooped to examine the ground.

"See anything?"

"I'm not sure." He got down on his hands and knees and ran his fingers across the grass. He stood up holding something.

"What is it?"

"A small piece of rubber." He showed her a two-inch square of thin rubber sheeting. "Odd."

"Do you think it means anything?"

"Help me find more pieces."

"Oh, Lord. You know I have a phobia against weeds. Look at the dandelions." They both got down on their hands and knees and bent over with their faces inches above the grass.

In ten minutes they were able to find a dozen minute pieces of rubber spread out in a pattern with a circumference of twenty feet. Lyon mentally noted where they had been found and looked up into the tree limbs that stretched overhead.

"I think I see it," he said finally.

"See what?"

"Let me make sure." He walked to a nearby oak and leaped to grasp a low limb. He swung his feet over the branch and pulled himself up. He held on to the trunk and reached for a higher limb.

"Your last involvement with a tree was a disaster."

"I won't fall."

"The tree you cut down didn't fall in the right direction either."

Lyon found what he was looking for thirty feet above the ground. Wound around a medium-sized limb was a thin wire. Attached to the end of the wire was a small rubber snout. He reached for the wire, lost his footing, and swung out over open space with one hand clutching the limb.

"Lyon!"

"I'm all right." He regained his footing on a lower branch. He'd seen enough of the wire to guess at its use. "Coming down." He began a careful descent to the ground and an apprehensive Bea. "I need a dog."

"What kind of dog?"

"Any grown male will do."

"Wentworth! Are you really asking me to go get you a dog?"

"It wouldn't have to be exclusively mine. We have been talking about getting one."

"Are you serious?"

"Couldn't be more."

She trooped off toward the car. "A dog. Why not? Why do I get involved in these things?" She climbed into the Datsun and drove away.

Lyon walked back toward the house until he was directly below the murder-room window. The house wall was sheer to the second floor and the small ornamental balcony at Serena's window. He stepped back until he had a full view of the complete side of the house. Above the balcony the wall continued upward to the slate roof without interruption. The nearest window in the third story of the house was a narrow affair near the roof. It was ten feet to the side of Serena's balcony.

He sat back against a tree, a stalk of grass in his mouth. He remembered a time decades ago in a foreign and forlorn landscape. He felt the harsh wind that blew off the Korean hills and shivered as he recalled its chill of death.

He had sat and watched then, perched for hours in forward positions observing what could be seen of the enemy's positions. He had placed himself in their minds as he attempted to fathom the unfathomable puzzle of war.

These murders were a war of a different sort. Men and women, good and bad, had died.

Lyon Wentworth looked toward the dead woman's room and plotted murder.

He didn't hear her approach until her arrival was announced by a deep *woof*. Bea clutched a heavy chain leash that was attached to a very large dog.

Another *woof*.

"I said a dog. Not a horse."

"Isn't he beautiful?" Bea ran a hand along the fawn-colored flanks of the Dane.

"Where did you get him?"

"At the animal shelter. He outgrew his owner's three-room apartment." The dog strained at the leash. His nose pointed toward the far wall at the edge of the grounds. "His father was a champion. His name is Count Nikolaus Von Zinzendorf. I thought we'd call him Nicky."

The dog tore the leash from Bea's hand and ran. He loped away from them in large bounds and headed toward the wall. "I hope the gate is closed," Lyon said as the dog disappeared into a small grove of trees.

"It is."

"I have a pretty good idea where he's going. Let's see."

They set off after the dog and found him at the grassy spot where the dead attack dog had been discovered on the previous day. The Dane was sniffing the ground and turning frantically in a small circle.

"It's the same scent that attracted the dog yesterday."

"I had always heard that a trained attack dog would never leave his handler or eat food offered by anyone else."

"That's a trained dog. I'll lay you ten to one that Smelts obtained that dog for Serena—cheap. He probably billed her for a trained attack dog and obtained one from God knows where."

"Untrained?"

"From the pound. You can take the dog back now," Lyon said as he started back to the house. "I want to take a look around inside."

"Wentworth! Wait a minute!" Bea grabbed the dog's loose leash and pulled the choke collar tight. She struggled after Lyon while pulling the recalcitrant dog. "Do you mean to say you wanted a dog for one measly test like that?"

"I wanted to verify my assumption." He turned to her in shock. "You mean you thought we'd keep him?"

"You said you needed a dog, so I got a dog complete with papers."

Lyon looked at the large animal sitting by Bea's side. His haunches were splayed to the side in that odd sitting position of a Great Dane. "Looks like a nice pooch," he said before turning to go back to the house.

"Oh, my God!" Bea slapped her forehead. "What I wouldn't give to be back in the state senate where at least the insanity is formalized." She jerked the leash. "Come on, Nicky. Follow that man."

A carpenter was at work repairing the murder-room door as Lyon entered. The room was a disaster area. Rocco's men and state police had moved and overturned furniture. A thin layer of plaster dust filmed all the uncovered surfaces. They had driven spikes into the thick walls in an attempt to locate a possible alternate entrance. He went into the bathroom, knelt by the tub, and turned the faucet on and off several times before leaving it on to allow a flow of hot water to fill the tub and spew steam into the air.

"I left Nicky tied downstairs," Bea said.

He let the stopper down and watched the flow of water slowly fill the tub: "Can I borrow your watch?"

"I didn't wear it this morning. You know, I gave you a watch for Christmas three years ago."

"I need a clock with a second hand on it." He left the bathroom and searched the room. The only clock available in the murder room was a clock-radio built into the bed's headboard. He stepped back into the hall and entered the room next door. It was a masculine bedroom with deep chairs and heavy carpeting. There was a small electric clock on the night table which he unplugged and took back into the bathroom. He replugged it into the electrical outlet on the wall next to the medicine chest.

"Checking the time it takes the tub to fill and overflow?" Bea asked.

"Yes. There's good pressure in the pipe system. It won't take long."

They both watched the filling tub as the water level rose gradually. Small rivulets of steaming water brimmed the top of the tub and began to seep across the floor. They backtracked from the room as the small streams fought their way toward the bedroom door.

"There must be a nearly imperceptible slant to the floor," Bea said.

"The house probably settled years ago."

The instant the crest of water reached the bedroom door, Lyon turned off the tub. He glanced at the small clock on the sink. "What time does that clock in the headboard read?"

"Eleven fifteen."

"This one's an hour behind."

"What does that mean?"

"I'm not sure."

"How long did the water take?"

"Eight minutes."

"That's within the time span."

"I know."

Lyon walked over to the French doors leading out to the small balcony and began to inspect the windowpanes closely. Bea righted an easy chair in the corner and sat down to observe her husband over folded hands. He was completely absorbed in his thorough examination. She often wondered how her eccentric husband, who often forgot to wear socks, was able to bring every particle of his conscious mind to bear on the problem of murder. There were strange currents within this man that after all these years she barely understood. He pulled a small bench from the dressing table to stand on and see the door's upper panes.

"Find anything?"

"I think so." He turned with a wry smile. "Let's look at the rest of the house."

He took her hand as they walked through the large house. Occasionally Lyon would leave her side and examine a door, a wall, or an odd piece of furniture.

"We're not going to buy the place, you know," she said.

"I would hope not. I find it oppressive."

They stood in the living room where they had had cocktails at the time of the murder. Lyon walked to the telephone and lifted the receiver. He dialed random single numbers.

"Serena called Ramsey. He spoke to her for a few moments and then hung up. We talked for a few minutes in here and then went down the hall to the dining room." Lyon walked into the hall with

Bea following as he made his way slowly to the dining room. "Were we alone?"

"I think you and I were the first ones to arrive in the dining room."

"It took a few minutes for the others to straggle in."

"Barbara Rustman stopped at the powder room while Ramsey stepped into the kitchen. He probably had some last-minute instructions for the cook."

"That's how I recall it. Still, we were all together a few minutes later."

"It couldn't have been even five. That's not time enough for someone to rush upstairs, enter Serena's room, and kill her in that manner before returning to the dining room."

"And that assumes the cooperation of Horace at the hall door and some way of getting through a locked door."

"Which means that whoever killed her had to go through the French doors on the balcony."

"Which were latched from the inside and guarded by a man on the outside below the window."

"Entering the murder room from the outside would assume the cooperation of the exterior guard. The murderer would have had to leave the rest of us in the living room, obtain a ladder or some such thing, and . . . No, it doesn't work."

"Very simple, Lyon. We were present at a murder that couldn't have happened."

"It would seem so. You know, I'd like to see the attic and the cellar."

"The cellar in this place must have rats. You can check that one out for yourself."

"There's probably an entrance from the kitchen." Lyon left Bea in the dining room and then disappeared into the recesses of the house.

"Anybody here!" A loud call from the hall.

Bea went to meet Rocco Herbert at the door. "Your playmate is exploring," she said.

"He can stop. The case is closed."
"Closed? How come?"
"We found Marty Rustman."
"He confessed."
"Hardly. He's quite dead."

13

WOLF PIT ROAD arches its way up from Route 90 and then wanders along a ridge line on the outskirts of Murphysville. It is a heavily wooded area that overlooks much of the river valley. Lyon had often wondered why home developers hadn't desecrated it. Perhaps the cost of cutting into the rock for lot sites made it prohibitive. Economics had to be why the area had not been raped. Aesthetic reasons never impeded avarice.

"When was the body found?"

"Early this morning," Rocco replied as he took a switchback turn too fast, causing the car to sway. "The body was burned beyond recognition, but I had a hunch and the ME's office ran the dental work against Rustman's."

"ID conclusive?"

"Hold up in any court in the land."

"The car?"

"Stolen yesterday from a supermarket parking lot. Actually, it was a pickup truck."

"Was?"

"You'll see." Rocco parked the police cruiser on the shoulder of the road and both men climbed out. They stood looking over the slim guardrail now shattered along a thirty-foot stretch. The charred remains of a pickup truck were canted obscenely far down the embankment.

"I'd like to take a look."

"Not much to see. Rustman had bad luck stealing that one."

"How's that?"

"It was loaded with oil drums. Come on, I'll show you."

They worked their way awkwardly down the embankment until they came to the burned truck. It was hardly recognizable as a motor vehicle. It was burned so extensively that paint had peeled off and any flammable item within the cab had been destroyed. All the windows had shattered.

"He stole the truck," Rocco said, "and was probably driving up here to hide for the night. He took the curve too fast and lost control. When he crashed through the guardrail, he might possibly have survived if the thing hadn't burst into flames. Isolated as it is up here, we didn't discover it until early this morning. It was difficult to identify the body as human."

Lyon winced. "What did the doctor say?"

Rocco shrugged. "What's to say. I saw it, Lyon. Believe me, you wouldn't care to."

"Are they going to run tests on the body?"

"I don't think so. Cause of death seemed obvious."

Lyon nodded and began to work his way up the hill to the road. At the top, he turned to extend his hand to Rocco and pull the panting chief up the last remaining feet. "You're closing the case?"

"Yep. This one saved the state some money."

"Let's have a drink."

"Sarge's Place?"

"Right."

BEA SAT IN HER CAR in the Rustmans' driveway. She was beginning to think that she was physically incapable of opening the door and going down the walk to ring the bell. How do you tell someone her husband is dead? How do you inform children that they have no father?

Rocco had asked her to do it and it had to be done.

She left the car, walked briskly up the path, and without hesitation pushed the bell. Barbara Rustman opened the door. Her features seemed to dissolve when her eyes met Bea's. Her hands fluttered and ran along her cheeks. "He's dead."

"Yes."

"I knew it."

"Are the children here?"

Barbara looked at her without comprehension. "The children?"

"Are they at home?"

"No, they aren't here. They're at the playground."

"Can I call someone for you?"

"Come in. Would you like coffee or something?"

"No, thank you."

They went into the small living room and sat at opposite ends of the couch. "How did it happen?"

"He was driving a pickup truck that ran off the road in Murphysville."

"Oh." The word was an expression of finality. "I didn't even know they made pickup trucks with those gadgets, but I suppose they do."

"I'm sorry to tell you the truck was stolen." Bea paused a moment. "What sort of gadget?"

"The kind the Veterans Administration put on Marty's cars."

"The VA? I don't understand."

"Marty was wounded in Vietnam. He didn't have much feeling in his right leg. All our cars had a hand throttle off the steering wheel. The government always paid for it."

"Could he drive a car or truck without the throttle?"

"I don't think so. He's dead now. That explains why he never called the children. I should have known."

"Is there anything I can do?"

"No. Thank you. I'll call our parents in a minute or two. You know, Marty was always afraid something would happen to him. He talked to me lots of times about what might happen and how it might look like an accident. That's why he told me where the money was."

"What money?"

"The money at the union hall. He said if he didn't come back, that after a day or two I was to go to the union hall and take the money from its hiding place. I did like he told me, but that man had me watched and found out. He knew I did it."

"Tanner. Gustav Tanner of the nursing home?"

"Yes. When the money was missing he called me. He said he knew I had it, that his man had seen me sneak into the hall. He said he would go to the police unless I . . . unless I . . ."

"Went to the motel with him."

"I went."

Barbara Rustman turned her head toward the cushions as cries racked her body. For the second time Bea went to the other woman and held her.

She was halfway to Murphysville before she realized the significance of the visit. She pulled the car off the shoulder and went to an open phone booth. She knew where Lyon would be and dialed the number of Sarge's Place.

CAPTAIN NORBERT OF THE state police was an unhappy man. Although he was pleased that his brother-in-law, Rocco, was also in police work, he was suspicious of the chief's friends. Not only did Lyon Wentworth write books but he also read them. Not only was Bea prominent in politics but she was also a Democrat. All of this made the husband-wife combination suspect. He wouldn't be surprised if they were closet Commies. Their kind usually were.

The chief and his friend were in their usual booth in the far corner of Sarge's Place. The scene made Norbert angrier, for he felt that if the major caught him in here, he'd be transferred to dormant records. He grimaced and pulled a straight chair over to the booth.

"Glad you could make it, Norbie," Rocco said.

"It better be important. I've got one hell of a lot of work to do to close this Rustman matter. We're having a news conference at five. You ought to be there, Chief."

"I'm surprised you told me about it."

Lyon twirled his pony of sherry. "I wouldn't do that if I were you."

"The major believes in being fair," Norbert said. "The case is solved, which makes Herbert and us look good."

"You're going to look foolish when you have to reopen it."

Lyon took the opportunity during the foreboding silence to signal Sarge for another drink. Captain Norbert's physical condition worried him. The man's complexion changed while they watched. His naturally florid face turned a deep hue of red as the color spread upward from the base of his neck. Rocco took the news more prosaically and merely shook his head.

"You had better explain yourself, Wentworth."

"He's been right before," Rocco said softly.

"He's always meddling in areas that civilians should stay out of."

"Rustman didn't do it," Lyon said and took the refilled pony from Sarge and smiled thanks.

"Like hell!" Norbert half rose from his chair. "The guy was a nut. Rustman's been running over the whole damn county knocking people off. He worked his way up until he got the woman and then ran the truck off the road."

"It fits the facts," Rocco added. "Everyone else in the house has been accounted for. Rustman could have come over the wall, killed the dog, and sneaked into the house. He somehow got into Serena's room and killed her. The only problem is that I'll be damned if I know how he got in and out of the room."

"Bea called me a few minutes ago," Lyon said. "She's been out to see Barbara Rustman. You can verify this with the Veterans Administration, but Marty Rustman was wounded in Vietnam and only had partial use of his right leg."

"He was limber enough to climb over that wall."

"Doubtful but possible. That pickup you found with his body, did it have hand controls?"

"No."

"Disabled veteran plates?"

"It had some sort of crazy vanity plates that spelled out 'Mary-Lou' or something like that. I can find out exactly."

"It won't be necessary. I'm convinced that Rustman's been dead since the day he disappeared."

"No one else could have killed Serena Truman."

"Someone did and I know how."

"This is the biggest bunch of crap I've heard all day." Norbert pushed away from the table. "I've got work to do."

"The major will be displeased if Lyon is right and you are wrong, Norbie."

The state police captain looked uncertain. "All right. I'll listen." He glanced at his watch. "For five minutes."

"It will take longer than that," Lyon said. "I'll show you how it was done."

"Show what?"

"How the murderer got into Serena's room and how the murder was committed."

"When?"

"Tomorrow night. Say seven. I'll need access to the mansion and two patrolmen to help."

"For God's sake, what am I going to tell the major?"

"That's your problem, Norbie," Rocco smiled.

SOL RABNER HATED shopping centers and discount stores with a passion that bordered on the irrational. He leaned against a counter in his downtown Murphysville store and watched his unmoving inventory with eyes of infinite sadness. A sixteen-year-old girl was the only potential customer in the shop, and Sol wasn't sure if she was prepared to buy or steal. He made a mental note to take a careful count of any items the girl took into the fitting room. He watched her from the corner of his eye and mentally calculated how much he should discount bathing suits.

A small bell hanging above the front door tinkled. Sol turned to see Lyon Wentworth enter. He smiled. The Wentworths were old customers. They didn't buy a great deal, and were frugal in their purchases, but they were consistent.

"Morning, Lyon."

"How's business, Sol?"

"The new shopping mall on Route Eighty really hurts. Nothing but low prices and shoddy merchandise. People don't appreciate quality anymore. What can I do for you?"

"I'm interested in that." Lyon pointed to a posed mannequin wearing a mauve evening dress.

Sol shook his head. "I really don't think that color would look good on Beatrice."

"Not the dress. The mannequin."

"The mannequin?"

"I want to borrow it for a few days. Better yet, I had better buy it. I think it might be destroyed."

"Wait a minute, Lyon. I'm not in the business of . . ."

"And I'll need something that comes in a large plastic bag."

"I have some nice cashmere sweaters that Beatrice might like."

"Fine. You pick out the size and color."

Sol Rabner shook his head. He began to strip the dress from the mannequin. The Wentworths were valued customers, but they were certainly strange.

BEA LOOKED UP from her gardening and pushed the floppy hat back on her forehead. Lyon's car came slowly down the driveway. A strange woman who didn't seem to be wearing any clothes was sitting next to him. She wondered what stray cat he had brought home this time. She walked over to the car as it stopped and leaned in the window.

"Your friend's got a rather vacant expression. Is she on something?"

"I bought you a sweater."

"At this time of year?"

"The price was right."

"Can I ask what you're doing?"

"I'm going to need your help. Did you get the other things?"

"They're in the study."

"Good."

Lyon slid from the car and hefted the mannequin over his shoulder. Bea followed him into the house and upstairs to the bedroom. He let the mannequin slip from his shoulder onto the bed and took the sweater from the plastic bag. "Tie my hands with a belt."

Bea shook her head. "You know I love you, Lyon, and we've had our good times together, but I'm not so sure that I'm into whatever it is you have in mind."

"It's only a rehearsal."

Bea arched an eyebrow.

THE POLICE HAD arrived at the mansion early. A state police cruiser and two Murphysville cars were parked in the drive when Lyon and Bea drove through the gate. Two trooper corporals in tailored uniforms stood nearby at attention. They looked with disapproval at two town police who lounged against the side of their car with loosened ties and dangling cigarettes. The divergent poses seemed to represent the chasm between the two police authorities.

Lyon parked near the entrance to the house and began to unload his equipment from the Datsun. Rocco came out the front door and smiled in wry bemusement as Captain Norbert shouldered past him and glared at the two Murphysville police who immediately straightened their posture and ground out their cigarettes.

"Morning, Senator," Norbert said with a salute to Bea before he turned to Lyon. "Now hurry it up, Wentworth. My men are on overtime."

"If you will allow me to arrange my props, then we can begin the reenactment."

"For Christ's sake, can I stop you?"

"No way," Rocco said.

The large dog strained against his choke collar as Bea led him from the car. She handed the leash to Jamie Martin. "I think he's your prop."

The officer took the leash with apprehension. "What am I going to do with him?"

"Lyon will tell you in his own good time."

"This is all costing the state money," Norbert snapped.

"I have something to do near the north wall," Lyon said. He heaved the mannequin out of the car and handed it to Rocco. "Will you take this up to the murder room and arrange her in bed?"

Rocco slung the mannequin over his shoulder. "Why not?" He started down the hall toward the main staircase.

Bea watched Rocco go up the stairs with the mannequin's naked legs protruding over his shoulder. "I can't make up my mind if he looks like Rhett Butler taking Scarlett upstairs or a Viking returning from a pillage of the English coast."

"Looks like a damn foolish cop to me," Norbert said.

"I'll be back in a few minutes." Lyon took an attaché case from the Datsun and began walking to the far wall.

"Couldn't he just diagram this for us, Senator?"

Bea watched her husband disappear behind the trees. "He has a theory, but whether it works out or not will depend on timing and your reaction."

LYON STOPPED AT THE spot near the wall where the guard dog had been poisoned. He sat cross-legged on the grass and gently lay the case flat on the ground before him. He unsnapped the clasps and opened the lid. Earlier that day he had dug out his wristwatch from the back of the bureau drawer and set the time by the radio. He glanced at the watch before he began his preparations.

When he and Bea had roamed the mansion in their attempt to understand how the murder was committed nearly all the details had puzzled him. Now, his experience with hot-air ballooning would be useful.

He went to work.

THEY CLUSTERED in the murder room looking down in macabre fascination at the mannequin in Serena's bed.

"Are the French doors latched, Rocco?"

Rocco checked the latch. "Yes."

"The bedside lamp is out. The water is not running in the tub."

"We all know that, Wentworth," Norbert said.

"We can duplicate everything except locking the door from the inside."

"We'll pretend."

"Fine." Lyon moved into the hallway. "I would like a police officer stationed in the hall immediately outside the bedroom door. I don't want anyone admitted into the murder room once the door is closed, and I want him to report anything he hears or sees to Rocco by walkie-talkie."

Rocco nodded toward a uniformed officer. "Got that, Hansen?"

"Yes, sir."

"Remember, notify the chief of anything you hear or see."

Lyon led them to the living room downstairs. Norbert paced the rug impatiently. "I would like Jamie Martin to walk the same guard post as the security man did below Serena's window. He must have the dog with him."

Rocco gestured to the patrolman who stood uncomfortably holding the dog on the leash. "You know the spot. I assume Lyon wants you to report on the radio anything you see or hear."

"Right, Chief. What about the dog?"

"Keep him with you," Lyon said. "But no matter what happens, do not leave your post."

Jamie led the dog gingerly down the hall and out the door.

"What in hell's going on?" Ramsey Mclean said as he strode into the living room accompanied by a short, bespectacled man holding a clipboard. "I thought you were through with the house, Chief?"

"What are you doing here, McLean?"

"We're taking an inventory for the estate."

"Wentworth has some scheme as to how the murder took place."

"I thought you found Rustman dead?"

"We did. There's still the problem of how he did it."

Ramsey turned to the man with the clipboard. "Why don't you

continue without me for a few minutes, Mr. Brumby? I'm quite interested in Mr. Wentworth's theory."

"I'll start on the silver in the pantry."

Ramsey was angry as Brumby left. "I want to know exactly what's going on."

"Lyon is going to duplicate the murder. Isn't that right?" Rocco said.

"Yes."

"We have a man posted in the hall outside your wife's room and a man with a dog outside. We have tried to approximate the circumstances as nearly as possible."

"Get on with it, Wentworth."

Lyon looked at his watch. "On the day of the murder Bea and I were working in the study. Will everyone please go in there. Rocco, if you will monitor any calls from the police on guard and please take notes, we'll begin."

"Does neatness count?"

"Funny."

Lyon stood in the center of the living room until Bea led the remaining police officers and Ramsey into the study. Once they were out of sight, he went into the pantry, past the man with the clipboard, and continued into the kitchen to the cellar door. He found a light switch near the stairwell and went down the open wooden stairs. He found the rope where he had discovered it yesterday, stuffed into an ancient coal bucket. It had been dyed brown, the same color as the outer walls of the house, and it was stout enough to support the weight of a man. He looped it over his shoulder and glanced at his watch.

Five minutes remaining.

The fuse box was next. It was a large wooden affair that was probably installed when the house was first constructed in the thirties. He counted three from the right on the second line, unscrewed a fuse, and stuck it into his pocket.

Four minutes left.

The water turn-off valves were neatly labeled with hanging white tags. He turned the appropriate valve and sprinted for the stairs. He took the cellar steps two at a time and raced for the servants' staircase that led from the kitchen to the third floor.

He entered a musty unused servant's room, tied an end of the rope to a heavy radiator, and stood with his back against the wall as he watched the second hand on his watch sweep around the dial. He thought again, as he had the day before, about the plight of men and women sentenced to these cell-like rooms for their working lives, on call most of the hours of the day, living without family six days a week. It was modern serfdom, which prosperity had finally destroyed.

He glanced at his watch again. Barely a minute left if his calculations were correct. Finding the bits of thin rubber on the grass where the dog had died had bothered him at first, and he had almost discarded them as possible clues until he discovered the rubber nipple high in the tree. If he made the assumption that no one had come over the wall and thrown the scented and poisoned meat on the ground to distract and kill the dog, the meat would have to have been hidden nearby in a sealed container until it was dropped at a specified time.

Earlier today he had duplicated the timing device and hung it in the tree. He had placed a thin string of sausage heavily doused with female dog musk inside a small weather balloon. Also inserted in the balloon was a small alcohol lamp. He had filled the balloon with air and ignited the lamp before he hung it high in a tree.

Seconds left. He pressed against the wall as near to the window as he dared and listened.

The pop was nearly inaudible at this distance, and more than likely the patrolling policeman outside would not have heard it.

The flame heated the air inside the balloon to the point where it expanded enough to explode the balloon. Small pieces of rubber had now fallen to the ground along with the scented meat.

He could hear the frantic bark of the Great Dane.

Lyon opened the narrow window, threw out the rope, and hoisted himself onto the sill. As he expected, Jamie Martin below was fighting to hold on to the Dane.

The dog made a final plunge and ripped the leash from the officer's hand and loped across the grass toward the trees at the far side of the grounds.

Lyon lowered himself onto the balcony, slipped chewing gum from his mouth, and placed it against a windowpane. The pane was held only loosely by a splotch of putty and it easily worked loose. He put the glass in his shirt and looped a thin strand of wire through the aperture and down over the latch of the French doors. He pulled on the wire and raised the latch.

In seconds he was inside the room with the doors shut behind him. A quick glance over his shoulder informed him that the officer below the window was looking bewilderedly after the Dane, unsure whether to give chase or remain at his post. He began talking over his radio.

Lyon removed the mannequin from the bed after tying a plastic bag over its head.

He placed the mannequin in the tub and turned on the hot water faucet all the way. A small trickle of water from inside the pipe drained into the tub for a moment and then stopped.

Back in the bedroom he turned on the switch for the bedside light.

He took a last look around the room. There was one more thing to be done. It was risky, but if he could do it soundlessly, it would be the final touch. He went to the bedroom door and turned the key in the door to the lock position.

The return to the third floor would be the most difficult part of the reenactment.

He pressed against the wall to watch the patrolman walk his post below the window. As he expected, the young officer, like most people, took a regular course that he duplicated constantly. He marched in military fashion from one end of the house to the other. Lyon waited until he passed the window and was going toward the front of the house. His back was now to the window.

Lyon slipped out the French doors and closed them behind him. He looped the wire back through the window where the pane was missing and latched the door. He replaced the pane easily and held it secure with chewing gum. He grasped the rope that he had looped around the balcony struts and swung out over the building and began his climb back into the servants' quarters.

He pulled the rope up after himself, shut the narrow window, and walked quietly down the backstairs and into the study.

"Anything from your men?" he asked Rocco.

"All quiet upstairs, but Jamie outside lost your dog."

"The gate's closed and he can't leave the grounds."

"What now?"

"We wait for the murder in the living room over drinks."

14

"WHEN DOES THIS murder take place?"

Lyon sank into an easy chair and tented his fingers. "Cocktails were served that day at seven."

"Wait a minute!" Captain Norbert was on his feet shaking in anger. "I've got two men on overtime." The corporals smirked. "We're not having any booze."

"We'll simulate the cocktails," Lyon replied.

"Then let's simulate that it's after seven."

Lyon stood up. "Everyone has a cocktail. Present are Bea and I, Ramsey, Mrs. Rustman, Tanner, and Smelts."

Rocco looked down at his nonexistent drink. "They make a lousy cocktail here."

"Serena called Ramsey at eight," Bea said.

"Can I simulate that?" Ramsey said. "Consider the call made."

"No. Go through the motions."

"Why not?" Ramsey walked over to the table with the phone. "We have a house intercom system. Serena dialed seven from her room, which would ring the phone in here. The phone rang and I picked it up."

"Please duplicate your conversation as best you can remember."

Ramsey held the receiver in his hand and looked thoughtful. "She said she had overslept and that she would be late. I told her it was nearly eight and dinner was ready. She told me to go ahead

159

and start with the others and that she would be down later after she bathed. Something along those lines."

"Good," Lyon said. "Tell me, Ramsey. When you talked to your wife, are you sure it was her?"

"Well, she mumbled a bit. Like she had just awakened. That wasn't unusual. She'd often take a nap in the afternoon and then stay up half the night."

"Could someone else have called from her room?"

"Well, yes. It could have been someone else. I assumed it was Serena."

"I see. Now, on the day of the murder, conversation continued in this room for a few minutes after Serena's call. Then dinner was announced."

"Serena always did like to be fashionably late for meals."

"All right," Lyon continued. "Dinner has now been announced and we all move into the dining room."

"Can we simulate that too?"

"Absolutely not. Please move in a leisurely fashion down the hall to the dining room."

The group ambled sheepishly down the hall. Bea started to stay by Lyon's side, but he waved her on and left the room last. He followed them down the hall but kept well to their rear. When the last police officer had entered the large dining room, he turned, went through the pantry door, and sprinted for the cellar steps. It took him forty seconds to reach the fuse box and screw the fuse back in and turn on the water for the upstairs bath. In another ten seconds he was back in the dining room. He took a seat at the table next to Bea.

Rocco's radio beeped. He answered in a voice too low for the others seated at the table to hear.

"Don't keep it a damn secret!" Norbert said when Rocco replaced the radio on his belt. "What in hell did he say?"

"Them. Both officers called. Hansen, in the upstairs hall, heard the water turn on and Jamie, outside, saw the bedroom light flick on."

"How'd you do that, Wentworth?"

"The same way anyone else who knew the house could have."

"McLean!" Rocco tumbled his chair backward as he catapulted to his feet. "Where in hell is he?"

"He was with us in the living room," Bea said. "I thought he came down the hall with us."

"He's the one, isn't he?"

Lyon nodded. "I think you should find him before he leaves the grounds."

Rocco barked into the radio. "Jamie! Hold Ramsey McLean. Don't let him leave."

Mr. Brumby, with his clipboard, poked his head in the door. "Mr. McLean just left. He said for you all to enjoy yourselves."

"Goddamn it!" Rocco slapped his thigh. He snatched the radio from his belt. "Do you see him, Jamie?" He glanced over at Captain Norbert. "He's made it through the gate."

Both senior police officers ran for the door. They reached their cars simultaneously and gave quick and concise orders over their car radios. Rocco finished first, took a map from the glove compartment, and spread it over the hood of the cruiser.

"I've got three cars operating this shift, and I've asked the two men at headquarters to use a spare vehicle to cover Route Eighty."

Norbert jabbed at the map. "We'll have roadblocks at both Murphysville ramps to the interstate within three minutes. The barracks is alerting the adjoining towns."

"He's only got a few minutes headstart. He'll never make it out of town." Rocco thumped a fist on the car hood. "We'll get the bastard." His radio beeped on his belt and he flipped it to receive.

"There's water coming under the door," Hansen yelled in excitement.

"I WISH IT WERE OVER."

They were gathered to wait at Nutmeg Hill. Lyon, sitting in his desk chair, swiveled to face Bea and Kim. Mandy Summers had seemed uncomfortable working in their presence, declined a drink, and left for a quiet spot in the upstairs guest room to proofread Lyon's book.

"Anyone hungry?" Bea asked. At the negative response she began to mix drinks at the bar cart. "I was surprised that Rocco and Norbie could work so well together. After years of listening to their flack, it was a pleasure to watch two professionals performing in unison."

Kim glanced at her watch. "Didn't seem to do much good. It's been two hours already. They will call when they catch McLean, won't they?"

"Said they would," Lyon said as he accepted a sherry from Bea. The drink tasted lifeless and flat. "He knows how anxious we are."

"All right, Wentworth. We've had our drink and now we're ready for explanations."

"Let's wait until Rocco comes so that we can go over it all at once. How's the strike coming, Kim?"

"With Smelts and his monkeys out of the way we have a fighting chance again."

"From what I was told earlier," Bea said, "Smelts is going to be out of the way for a good long time."

A car raced up the drive and stopped by the front door. The hallway clump of large brogans made it obvious that Rocco had arrived. He entered the study without acknowledging their presence and mixed a strong vodka and water.

"We take it you've been unsuccessful," Kim said.

"You take it right," he replied and drained half the drink. "Bastard couldn't have slipped through unless he walked through the woods or swam the river."

"How about holing up somewhere?"

"That's always possible. He could be at a friend's house or might have broken into a vacant place. He'll have to come out eventually."

"You never found Rustman until he was killed."

"There wasn't any Rustman to find. Lyon was right. He'd been dead for days."

"He was already dead when the truck burned?"

"Yes. They hadn't intended to run further tests on the body until we alerted them to that possibility. The burning of the body was a subterfuge."

"He'd been dead all the time," Bea said.

"The medical examiner is now certain that he was."

"But the body . . . I mean it should have decomposed."

"My educated guess is that Rustman's body was hidden in the freezer at the Arcadia Produce Company by McLean and accidentally discovered by the manager," Lyon said.

"Which would account for the manager's death," Rocco added.

"All right, Lyon," Bea said. "Let's hear it. Rocco will get Ramsey eventually, but I want to know the rest of it."

"From the top?"

"A fine place to start."

"The death of Dr. Bunting was never intended."

"She had the misfortune of seeing them snatch Marty," Kim said.

"Exactly. She was murdered by Maginacolda for what she saw. Rustman was killed in the state forest not only for his opposition to Smelts's union, but also because he had evidence on its illegal connection with the Shopton Corporation."

"And was dead the whole time?"

"I'm afraid so. The body was moved by Ramsey as part of his scheme."

"To make all the other deaths seem tied together."

"Yes. Ramsey knew that Rustman was going to be kidnapped, and it was easy enough for him to find out where he had been killed and buried. He moved the body and then killed Maginacolda and Falconer."

"Why move Rustman's body?" Rocco asked. "As it was, we nearly didn't find it."

"A couple of reasons," Lyon said. "Smelts was still alive and knew where Rustman was buried. Also, unless he froze the corpse, the body's deterioration would have been immediately obvious to the assistant medical examiner."

"Okay," Rocco said. "And then he went after Smelts."

"All to make Serena more fearful for her own life. He knew she had a pathological fear of death by asphyxiation."

"But that only resulted in her sealing herself in the house surrounded by half a dozen guards."

"He had worked it out that way. I'm sure he not only encouraged Serena to increase her security, but he might even have suggested that Bea and I be present for that dinner party. We were to provide the iron-clad alibi for his presence during the supposed time of the murder."

"What about motive?"

"Greed and fear. He knew that Serena was going to end their marriage, which would preclude him from handling her future legal work. He also knew his wife well enough to know that eventually she would begin to worry about him and what he knew. Divorce would not be enough for Serena. She would arrange for Ramsey to have an accident."

"Kill him?"

"Probably."

"Which all leads to Serena's murder."

Rocco mixed another drink. "Run through the details on that one. I think I have most of it, but there are some holes."

Lyon leaned back in his swivel chair and extended his legs with his hands laced behind his head. "Ramsey had already suggested that Bea and I be brought to the mansion, but Serena's idea of confronting the others was gratuitous. It was a made-to-order situation for him with everyone who had a motive for murder present at the house."

"How did he get into the room?"

"The same way I did."

"But both guards heard and saw things. The light went on at eight and then the water ran in the tub."

"Ramsey had removed a fuse in the cellar and also turned off the water. When Serena was dead, he turned on the light switch and the water faucet. Later he replaced the fuse and turned the water back on."

"Wait a minute," Bea said. "When you and I were in the murder room, you got a clock from the room next door. It was an hour behind."

"Ramsey was astute enough to set the clock in the murder room ahead for the length of time he knew the electricity would be off. Evidently he didn't realize that the room next door was on the same circuit. That's what alerted me to the possibility of how it was done."

"Then who was his accomplice?" Kim asked.

"There wasn't one."

"Ah ha," the black woman chortled. "There had to be. Your reenactment has a hole big enough to drive a truck through."

"How's that?"

"The phone call. You tell us Serena was dead long before eight, but someone called Ramsey McLean in the living room at eight. I can understand how he could pretend it was his wife on the line, but someone had to make that call."

"We all heard the phone ring," Bea added.

Lyon leaned across his desk and picked up the phone. "I assumed Ramsey was calling his answering service just before Serena supposedly called. He dialed, said something, and hung up." Lyon dialed a series of numbers on his phone and hung up. "After he did that, Ramsey turned to me and asked a question. I replied." The phone on Lyon's desk rang. He let it ring three times before picking it up. "Yes," he said into the receiver. "I understand . . . at eight . . . and so forth and so forth." He hung up.

"Who was it?" Bea asked.

"No one. I did the same thing that Ramsey did that day in the living room."

"A telephone repairman's callback," Rocco said.

"Exactly. When repairmen fix your phone, they have a certain number of digits that cause the phone to ring back on its own number after a five-second delay. In this phone district it's simple enough . . . your own phone number plus a repeat of the last digit."

"Ramsey didn't call his answering service. He was calling his own number."

"Right."

"And when the phone rang, he answered it and we all assumed it was Serena," Bea said.

"She was already dead," Rocco said.

"Yes. Then when we went in to dinner, Ramsey slipped back into the cellar to replace the fuse and turn on the water."

"Which gave the son of a bitch five witnesses to prove where he was during the time we thought the murder occurred."

"He was sure he was safe until today when he saw Lyon putting all the pieces together," Bea said.

"Which wraps it up," Rocco said. "If we could only get the guy."

"You will," Lyon said.

SHE KNEW IT WAS a dream because she wore her pink peignoir to the outdoor café. Others around her were formally dressed and Fabian Bunting sat across the small oval table sipping vermouth and smiling. Bea felt as if they had been talking for hours. It was a time long ago and yet near. She felt relieved that Fabian was much younger and still alive. A tall, cool drink was served by a faceless waiter and Bea leaned forward to ask her old teacher a dozen questions.

Faby Bunting stood and Bea knew she was going to leave. There was a wistful smile on Fabian's face. A smile not of sadness, but of fulfillment—it was over and Bea Wentworth's ghosts were leaving.

A cool wind swept down the Champs Élysées and she shivered and awakened.

Something was wrong. Lyon was sitting upright in bed next to her. She felt the tense muscles in his thigh as his leg pressed against her. She lay without sound or movement as her eyes adjusted to the dim light.

There was a dark bulk by Lyon's side of the bed. A man was leaning over her husband and pressing something against his forehead.

"What is it?" she asked.

"Ramsey" was Lyon's curt reply.

"Out of bed, both of you."

"He has a gun."

They slipped simultaneously from their respective sides and groped for clothing. Ramsey retreated to the far side of the room. His hand brushed along the wall until it encountered the overhead light switch and flipped it on. The room was suddenly bright.

If the man hadn't held an automatic pistol on them, Bea might have laughed. She and Lyon were on opposite sides of the room slipping into trousers. They each had one foot in one leg and looked up in embarrassment when the light flicked on.

"Hurry," Ramsey said.

Lyon zipped his pants and slipped into canvas boat shoes. "What are you going to do with us?"

"Have you drive me out of here."

"Then what?"

"Then we'll see. I can't think of a better couple to get me past Herbert's roadblocks."

Bea saw the Great Dane standing in the doorway behind Ramsey. The large dog's lips were pulled back to reveal long fangs as he gave a low growl. His head turned slowly one way and then the other. He would attack the intruder. His huge body would hurtle through the air and throw the man to the floor where Lyon could wrest the pistol from Ramsey's grasp.

Ramsey half turned and looked at the dog in the doorway. He reached his free hand back toward the animal. "Here, boy."

The dog lumbered over to the outstretched hand and licked the fingers. So much for that, Bea thought.

"Where are the car keys?" The pistol turned from one to the other.

"Hanging on the corkboard in the kitchen. We have a Datsun wagon and a pickup."

"The Datsun will do. Come on, downstairs." Ramsey stepped aside and motioned with the gun for them to walk ahead.

Lyon took her hand as they walked through the doorway together. They went down the stairs that way, walking as slowly as possible, afraid to reach the kitchen, find the keys, and go out to the car in the drive.

"Where have you been?" Lyon asked.

"In the pines not a hundred yards from your house."

"You hid your car in there?"

"Cut the chatter, Wentworth, and get me the keys."

"You've been watching the house all evening?"

"I saw Herbert and your black friend leave."

LYON KNEW he would kill them. He also knew that in the event they were stopped by a roadblock, Rocco would let them through. He would stall for time, but let them pass in the hope that somewhere further on a rescue could be made.

There would be no rescue. The man with the gun was desperate, cunning, and determined. He had killed so many times recently that two more would be insignificant.

"Hurry up! Damn it! The keys."

"I have them." Lyon slipped the car keys off the peg on the corkboard, and turned to face Ramsey, who was standing in the kitchen doorway.

Bea saw the movement behind their captor the instant Lyon did and stepped quickly to the side.

Mandy Summers and Rocco Herbert stood silently behind Ramsey. Rocco slid the Magnum from its holster and raised the heavy handgun with his left hand supporting the right until the barrel was inches from the rear of Ramsey's head.

Mandy's eyes were frightened. Lyon realized that the insomniac woman had been working in the spare bedroom all evening. She had undoubtedly seen the dark figure of McLean cross the side yard and heard him force his way into the house. She had phoned Rocco.

"You're going to kill us, aren't you?" Bea said.

"Not if you cooperate. Open the door, Beatrice."

Bea turned the latch on the side door. Her eyes never left the three people standing in the hall. Ramsey's gun was pointed directly at Lyon.

"Move and you're a dead man," Rocco's voice uttered a low and menacing command.

Ramsey's shoulder twitched, but his gun never wavered from Lyon. "Herbert?"

"Drop it, McLean," Rocco's voice was nearly a whisper.

"Your friend dies," Ramsey said. Lyon saw a small nerve in the man's chin twitching spasmodically.

"So do you." Rocco's voice dropped another register so that the words were barely audible to Bea and Lyon at the far side of the kitchen. Ramsey's eyes glistened in a combination of fright and blood lust.

Rocco was going to kill Ramsey. Lyon looked from the police chief's face to the strained countenance of the man aiming at him. Ramsey's face might be taut with tension, but the hand holding the automatic was steady.

Lyon suspected that he knew more about weapons than the murderer did. Rocco would fire, and the huge muzzle velocity of the Magnum would knock Ramsey from his feet and kill him instantly. He might be able to fire at Lyon, but the odds were excellent that the impact of the killing bullet would deflect his shot. Handguns at any range are notoriously inaccurate, but Rocco was too close to miss.

Ramsey McLean would die, and perhaps there was a fitting justification to that. A life taken in some ancient code of retribution.

It could not happen. It must not happen.

"Rocco . . . Don't!" Lyon stepped toward Ramsey, directly into the muzzle blast of the automatic, as both guns fired simultaneously.

15

THE WHEELS OF THE stretcher creaked as it moved across the living-room carpet. It was pushed by men in white. Lyon turned his head to watch it approach. Death did not come in black. It arrived in white, worn by bored men who had seen it all.

He became aware of his body and tentatively stretched. His head hurt, but he was alive. His hand moved slowly toward his head to feel the damp cloth covering his forehead. His eyes focused up at Bea and Rocco as they hovered over the divan where he lay.

"I think I'm alive."

"You shouldn't be. You damn fool!" Rocco turned and walked into the kitchen.

"His bullet grazed your head," Bea said. "You better go to the emergency room and have it looked at."

"I'll be all right." He struggled to sit up and felt dizzy, but Bea's hands under his shoulders supported him. He swung his feet off the side of the couch and leaned back against the cushions until a wave of nausea passed.

Mandy Summers stood in the corner of the room looking at the body sprawled in the kitchen doorway. The ambulance attendants were arranging a body bag.

They watched the attendants who, with professional efficiency, rolled the body into the bag and lifted it onto the stretcher in one even motion. Lyon had a vivid picture of Ramsey, only minutes before, standing in the doorway. Now McLean was dead and he was alive. "What happened?"

"For some reason you stepped toward Ramsey and he fired. Rocco had to shoot. He didn't have any choice."

"I didn't mean for it to happen that way."

They were silent as the stretcher creaked across the room toward the door.

"The book is done, Mr. Wentworth," Mandy Summers said.

"What book?"

"The one I've been retyping. It's about these monsters called the Wobblies that . . ."

"I know what it's about, Mandy."

"I guess my job here is finished."

"I'm afraid I really don't have anything else for you to do."

"We want to thank you for what you did tonight, Mandy. You saved our lives."

"I thought it was that man when I saw him sneaking across the yard. You've both been very nice to me."

"You know, Mandy, I could arrange for you to have an interview with the state personnel department. They need people with your skills."

"Thank you, but I tried that, Mrs. Wentworth. They won't hire anyone who's a convincted felon."

"I believe I could arrange a waiver for you."

"Could you?" For the first time since they had known her, Mandy Summers' face showed vestiges of animation.

"I think I can guarantee it."

A deep series of barks from outside the house interspersed with male cursing precluded all further conversation. Lyon started for the door, but stopped at the edge of the couch as a wave of dizziness broke over him. "That dog's got to go."

Kim Ward entered the house holding on to the Dane's collar. "Your hound almost ate two attendants and one ambulance." She let go of the collar. "Are you two all right?"

"Lyon's going to have a headache, but yes, we're all right."

"Was Rocco the one who . . . ?"

"Rocco killed him," Lyon said softly.

"How is he?"

"Seems all right."

For the first time they became aware of the scraping sound from the kitchen. Lyon walked toward the kitchen door and grabbed the edge of the stove to steady himself. "My God, Rocco! Don't do that."

His oldest friend didn't answer. Rocco Herbert was down on his hands and knees by the kitchen wall where Ramsey McLean had once stood. He had a bucket of soapy water by his side and was vehemently scrubbing the bloodstained floor with a stiff brush. He didn't look up.

Bea whispered in Lyon's ear. "What's he doing?"

"Rocco, stop that."

"I killed him" was the chief's reply.

"You had to. You saved our lives."

"Yes, I had to." The reply was nearly inaudible.

Bea looked at Lyon with a significance that didn't need expression. She crossed the room and bent down near the sink to rummage through a cabinet. She found another brush, knelt next to Rocco, and began to scrub.

Lyon braced his back against the wall as he watched his wife and friend desperately try to remove the bloodstains.

He wanted to cry but knew it wouldn't help. He knelt next to them to help scrub.